9.99

PARTY HOST OR PARTY GHOST?

Jane saw a wisp of white in the shadows and quickly moved the beam of her light toward it in time to see something or someone disappear through the opened back door into the night.

"She went outside," she said, hurrying toward the opening.

"Where's she going?" Hillary called to her.

"Look! She just went into that little house there."

They reached the house, both with muddy, wet feet, and when they were inside, Jane swept the small beam of the flashlight around.

"Looks like a garden shed," Hillary said. "And it looks like the ghost has disappeared again."

Jane continued to shine her light around the room. "She's got to be in here somewhere," she said, in spite of the fact that no one, other than the two of them, was visible. Suddenly she felt something flying past her head and in almost the same second heard a thud. She turned quickly to see the yellow handles of a pair of large gardening shears still quivering from having been thrust into the wall. They had been thrown from somewhere in the darkness, and they had been meant for her head. . . .

DEATHDAY
PARTY

WITHDRAWN

PAULA CARTER

BERKLEY PRIME CRIME, NEW YORK

DEATHDAY PARTY

A Berkley Prime Crime Book / published by arrangement with the author

PRINTING HISTORY
Berkley Prime Crime mass-market edition / October 1999

All rights reserved.
Copyright © 1999 by The Berkley Publishing Group.
This book may not be reproduced in whole or in part,
by mimeograph or any other means, without permission.
For information address: The Berkley Publishing Group,
a division of Penguin Putnam Inc.,
375 Hudson Street, New York, New York 10014.

The Penguin Putnam Inc. World Wide Web site address is
http://www.penguinputnam.com

ISBN: 0-425-17121-3

Berkley Prime Crime Books are published
by The Berkley Publishing Group,
a division of Penguin Putnam Inc.,
375 Hudson Street, New York, New York 10014.
The name BERKLEY PRIME CRIME and the BERKLEY PRIME CRIME
design are trademarks belonging to Penguin Putnam Inc.

PRINTED IN THE UNITED STATES OF AMERICA

10 9 8 7 6 5 4 3 2 1

DEATHDAY PARTY

1

Your career is about to take an interesting turn.
You may be getting that promotion you've
been looking for, but the path is fraught with
danger. Beware of the dead. Your love life is
on hold for a few days.

Jane Ferguson tossed the *Prosper Picayune* on her book-
strewn coffee table with a world-weary snort. She read the
horoscopes occasionally, mostly for amusement. She had to
admit, though, she always secretly wished that she would
see her own bright future under the section labeled Leo.
She had another reason for reading today's horoscope. Her
employer, Hillary Scarborough, had told her a few days ago
that they would be catering a big party for the Bean family
who lived back in the woods somewhere in Taladega
County, which was between Prosper and Birmingham. Cas-

sandra Bean was the author of the *Prosper Picayune*'s "Your Daily Horoscope" column. Today's horoscope predicted even more ridiculous events than usual.

For one thing, there was no way she was going to get a promotion. Being the only employee of Hillary Scarborough's company, Élégance du Sud, other than the receptionist, there was nowhere to go, unless Hillary made her a partner, which wasn't likely, and it was a position she wasn't sure she would want to accept, anyway. Jane was convinced she made more money as an employee than she would taking on the risks of ownership, and she needed as much money as she could get to support herself and Sarah. Ten-year-olds had a way of outgrowing clothes and consuming food at an alarming rate, and Jim Ed, her ex, wasn't exactly generous with his child support, in spite of the fact that he was now a big-shot civil litigation lawyer.

Élégance du Sud specialized in catering parties and events, which Hillary referred to as "affairs," and in home decorating. Jane's immaculately coiffed and manicured boss called it "interior design." She also had a weekly television show, which Jane produced, featuring either cooking, decorating, or gardening. Hillary thought of herself as the Martha Stewart of the South.

The second ludicrous item in today's horoscope was the mention of a love life, on hold or otherwise. Hers was virtually nonexistent. Jane had been asked out twice since her divorce, both times recently and both times by Beau Jackson, a detective in the Prosper, Alabama, police department. He'd broken the first date when he got called out on a domestic violence case, and she'd broken the second one when Sarah got a stomach bug.

The admonition to beware of the dead was, of course, the most absurd of all. Cassandra Bean was weird like that, though. If she could keep from throwing in little tidbits such as "the ghost of your father wishes you to know . . ." or "listen for the voice of Cleopatra, who wants to warn you about . . ." she might have a chance at national syndication, something like the late Jeane Dixon. For now, though, she was stuck with a daily column in Prosper, Alabama, along with one or two other small Alabama towns, where her biggest problem seemed to be convincing the local Fundamentalist religious community that she wasn't doing the work of the devil.

The phone rang and Jane began the search for it. She'd recently bought a cordless phone—a true luxury for her, since a few months ago she couldn't even pay her phone bill—but its portability meant she could never find it. She picked up the newspaper and tossed it aside, thinking the phone might be underneath it, but there was nothing there except the half-eaten bagel she'd been munching on last night before bed. The phone continued to screech at her in elongated exclamation points. The sound seemed to be coming from the desk. She stumbled across the shoes she'd kicked off last night after work and knocked over a Pepsi can on the coffee table. God only knew how long it had been there, she thought as what was left of the syrupy brown liquid spilled out. Jane used the bottom of her bathrobe to wipe it up with one hand while she continued searching with the other hand for the elusive phone, which called out with persistent urgency. She patted the mound of papers that cluttered the desk—some of them Sarah's schoolwork, some of her own, left over from last semester. She'd been in law school up until last semester, when she'd been forced by lack of money to drop out. Jim Ed was supposed to help her through law school in return for the three years she'd worked to help him get his law degree. Seems he'd gotten diverted from that promise when the former Miss Alabama came along.

Jane had meant to go through those old papers and sort them out months ago, but her work kept her busy. Housekeeping wasn't her forte anyway, although she did her best to hide that fact from Hillary, whose house was kept impeccable by a live-in maid.

Finally, she found the mound of papers that had been hiding the phone. Its red light blinked at her, impatient. She pressed the button and brought the phone to her ear.

''Hello.'' She was still dabbing at the syrupy spot on the coffee table.

"Jane? Is that you?"

"Yes, Hillary." It was Saturday. Jane was supposed to have the weekend off, but that never stopped Hillary. She had no aversion to calling on weekends or in the middle of the night, if the notion struck her. Jane was willing to put up with it for the freedom Hillary gave her; she had no set hours. She simply worked until the job was done, and Hillary was always generous and understanding about her need to be home when Sarah was there.

"Did I tell you that we're catering the Bean affair next week?" Her voice flowed with the sweet honey of a Southern accent.

"You told me, Hillary," Jane said. Her own accent was nondescript, California born and bred.

"Well, I was just thinking that maybe we ought to take a run out there today and have a look at the place. You know, get an idea of what kind of space we'll have for serving; how we should lay out the tables, that sort of thing. You can bring Sarah along if you want to."

"It's semester break. Sarah's spending a few days with her dad in Birmingham, and I have to be here until he comes to pick her up at nine."

"Well, all right, hon," Hillary said. "Just remember, it's going to take us a good while to get out to the Bean's, and I want to be back in time to get ready for the garden club dinner tonight, so we'll have to leave here around noon. I'll come pick you up."

"Oh no, Hillary, I don't mind driving. Why don't I pick you up?"

"Nonsense, lamb. We'll take the Cadillac. Billy says it's all tax-deductible anyway, when I drive it for business." Billy was her husband, whom Jane had yet to meet. He was always away, either on hunting or fishing trips or on business. Jane had never been sure what kind of business he was in, but it seemed to be lucrative, judging by the Scarboroughs' lifestyle.

"But Hillary, if I drive—"

The buzz of the dial tone interrupted her. Jane pushed

the hang-up button and sighed with what came close to a shudder. She glanced down at the newspaper, and her eyes fell upon the horoscope.

Your career is about to take an interesting turn. . . . The path is fraught with danger. . . .

Any time she rode in a car Hillary was driving, it was bound to be interesting and fraught with danger, more danger than Jane cared to experience. Maybe she should be grateful for the diversion. It would help keep her from missing Sarah so much.

"What's for breakfast, Mom?" Sarah bounced down the stairs, already dressed in jeans and a sweatshirt. The fact that she was dressed by eight o'clock on Saturday was a little disconcerting to Jane. The two of them usually lounged around in pajamas and robes until at least nine. Jane did her best to convince herself that it was all right for Sarah to be eager. Jim Ed was her father, and she loved him. He'd divorced Jane, not his daughter. She stood and placed an arm around Sarah's shoulders. Maybe her feelings were petty and possessive, she thought, but they were real, nevertheless.

"How about pancakes?" Jane's tone had a brightness to it she didn't feel.

"OK," Sarah said. "Just follow the recipe on the back of the Bisquick box, and be sure the griddle is hot enough before you pour the first one on. You know what I mean? A drop of water should sizzle."

She gave her daughter a playful pat on the bottom. "Oh, cut it out, Sarah. You're starting to sound like Hillary with all your little domestic hints."

Sarah giggled and touched her hair in one of Hillary Scarborough's mannerisms. "Well, ah declare, lamb," she drawled.

Jane laughed, but when they reached the kitchen, Sarah was pulling out the mixing bowl and the Bisquick box, ready to help.

"It's not that I think you can't do this, Mom. I just thought it would be fun if we did it together." Sarah sounded a little defensive as she went to the refrigerator for milk and eggs. Sarah knew her mother wasn't much better at cooking than she was at cleaning, Jane thought. "Besides, I don't get to do this when I go to Daddy's. Leslie Ann doesn't cook at all."

"She doesn't?" Jane wasn't really surprised. She'd never been able to visualize the twenty-four-year-old former Miss Alabama, who was now Jim Ed's wife, in the kitchen in the first place.

"No. She's really busy being a lawyer and helping Daddy try all those cases, but that's OK. They take me to really cool restaurants." She was trying to crack an egg on the side of the bowl.

"I'm sure they do. Here, let me do that, Sarah. You set the table."

"OK, but can I flip 'em?"

"Sure." Jane was scrutinizing the instructions carefully. Maybe she couldn't make her daughter proud by shining in the courtroom yet, and maybe she didn't wear a size six and have a perfect shape like Leslie Ann, but she could damn sure make pancakes from a prepared mix.

The pancakes were rubbery, but it had been fun making them. They sat down to eat at the old-fashioned chrome-trimmed table Jane had bought at a used furniture store after Jim Ed got all the furniture in the divorce settlement. It wasn't Hillary's gleaming porcelain and oak kitchen or her gourmet recipe, but that didn't spoil the happy mood that lasted even through the cleanup. Both were relaxed, Sarah telling her the latest playground gossip from school. Her best friend, Shakura Young, was going to have her tonsils out in a couple of weeks, and she thought Miss Weatherspoon, her violin teacher, had a boyfriend.

"A boyfriend? Really? Miss Weatherspoon? What makes you think so?" Miss Weatherspoon was a fifty-year-old spinster who made her living teaching piano and violin to Prosper's children. Tall and bony, plain and quiet. Not the type to have a boyfriend.

" 'Cause I heard her talking mushy on the phone once when I got there early for my lesson, and she has a new picture of some guy she keeps on the piano."

"Really? What does he look like?" Jane turned the knob to start the dishwasher and picked up a dish towel to dry the griddle she'd just cleaned. Sarah, though, had lost interest in the gossip and had wandered off to the living room to glance out the window, watching for her father's sports car while Jane changed into the new black leggings and tunic she'd bought at the local JC Penney a couple of weeks ago. She glanced at herself in the mirror, feeling chic. The outfit helped camouflage her slightly too wide hips.

It was almost nine-thirty before Jane saw Jim Ed Ferguson's Porsche pull into her driveway. It wasn't her ex-husband who was driving, but Jane recognized the attractive blond behind the wheel. She swung her long legs out of the low-slung car, grabbed a large, fashionable handbag from the seat, and took a moment to straighten her very small, very chic miniskirt before she strode up to the door with the long, gliding walk of a model.

"It's Leslie Ann!" Sarah sounded excited.

"Isn't it, though."

"I wonder why Daddy didn't come." Sarah seemed to ignore her mother's sarcasm, and Jane noted with a measure of relief that her question was more curiosity than disappointment.

"Maybe he just needed a little time to himself. I mean, a man can only stand so much perfection."

Still, Sarah ignored her. She hurried to the door and had it open before Leslie Ann could ring the doorbell.

"Hi, Leslie Ann!"

"Sarah!" Leslie Ann opened her arms and encircled

Sarah with them while a hint of White Shoulders, incongruously frilly and feminine, but quintessentially Southern, wafted into the living room.

They hugged each other like two best friends, then Leslie Ann reached into her oversized Gucci bag and pulled out a package. "I brought something for you," she said, handing the package to Sarah.

"Please come in," Jane said, feeling dowdy in the black leggings and tunic she'd felt so good about only a moment ago.

"Oh, I really don't have time," Leslie Ann said, in spite of the fact that she was coming in anyway. "Sarah and I are going to spend a little time shopping at the Galleria, and Jim Ed has made reservations for us tonight at the country club. We want to have that all done so Sarah can get to bed early. Have to take care of our little girl, you know." She stroked Sarah's long blond hair as Sarah tore at the wrapping paper.

"Our little girl?" Jane's uncomfortable question was drowned out by a screech of surprise as Sarah got the package open.

"It's a Barbie MasterCard," Leslie Ann said. "I thought you'd like it. See this little, tiny credit card? Isn't it cute? And you just run it through this little machine. Watch. Like this, and see! It says 'purchase approved.' Now isn't that darling?" Leslie Ann was beaming as she turned to Jane.

Jane felt as if she would choke if she tried to speak. She could only manage a weak smile. The only word she could think of anyway was "disgusting." Sarah, however, seemed to be intrigued with running the tiny credit card through the tiny machine and seeing the words "purchase approved" appearing over and over again. Maybe it was just the novelty of the thing. Jane hadn't used a credit card in months. She'd maxed out the card she had before she'd found a job, and she was still trying to whittle down the debt.

Leslie Ann was still beaming. "Oh, and wait until you see what I have for you at home, Sarah! No, no, I just can't wait that long.'' She gave a little giggle. "It's a poster of Leonardo DiCaprio!''

"No!'' Sarah was all but jumping with excitement.

"Yes!'' Leslie Ann squealed.

"That is sooo cool! Leonardo DiCaprio! Really?'' Sarah was beaming.

"Leonardo DiCaprio?'' Jane was puzzled.

"You know, *Titanic*? *Romeo and Juliet*?'' Leslie Ann seemed equally puzzled that Jane had to be told. "He is such a hunk!''

"Oh, yeah, the hunk.'' Jane turned to Sarah. I thought you liked Brad Pitt.

"Mom, he is *so* old.''

Leslie Ann giggled again. "Really.'' She glanced at Jane. "He is getting up there, you know. He's got to be five or six years older than I am.'' She'd said that as if being six years older than twenty-four was old.

Jane gave her another of her weak smiles.

"Well, we've got to be going. Is this your bag?''

"I'll get it.'' Jane gave it a tug. What had Sarah put in there? A ton of rocks?

"Oh no, don't bother. I can manage. You might hurt your back.'' Leslie Ann picked up the bag, her perfectly formed stick-slender arms showing no strain at all.

"See you Tuesday, Mommy.'' Sarah gave Jane a kiss on the cheek.

Jane held her close a little too long and let her hand trail after her as she ran to the car and slid into the bucket seat next to Leslie Ann. The two of them were chattering and laughing as they backed out of the driveway and started down the street.

Jane spent the morning slumped on the sofa, flipping through channels and running the Barbie credit card through its tiny machine while she mumbled in a mincing, mocking voice, "You might hurt your back!'' It was past one o'clock before she heard the sound of screeching tires and the click-clack of high heels on the driveway.

When the doorbell rang, she called over her shoulder, "Come in, Hillary. It's open.''

She turned around to see Hillary push the door open and step inside. Hillary looked around at Jane's cluttered living room. "My, my, I'm always amazed at how—well, casually—you live," she said. She was wearing a pair of autumn brown Liz Claiborne silk slacks with a matching sweater and shoes with short, narrow heels. Her voluptuous hair was perfectly coiffed and her nails manicured and mauved so that the tips of her fingers looked like a series of pale rose petals. She was well into her forties, although she never revealed either her age or her weight, and the well-to-do Southern belle look she cultivated seemed effortless.

Jane's only response to her was a disinterested shrug.

"Well, if you don't look like somebody just killed your best milk cow," Hillary said, looking at Jane still slumped on the sofa. Hillary studied her face carefully. "Jim Ed say something to upset you?"

Jane carefully put the Barbie credit card and machine on the coffee table and used the remote to turn off the television.

"I'm all right. Guess I'm always just a little depressed when Sarah leaves. And no, Jim Ed wasn't even here."

Hillary nodded knowingly. "Ah, but Miss Alabama was."

"Yeah, Miss Alabama, with her size-two miniskirt and her perfect body and her law degree, who knows more about my daughter's interests than I do."

"Do I detect a little jealousy?"

"Of course not." There was a pause. "Well, a little, maybe. She treated me like I'm old or something."

"Get over it."

"What?"

"I said get over it. Sarah's too smart to fall for that superficial stuff. And anyway, we've got work to do. That will take your mind off of all of this."

"We're just going to check this place out, right?" Jane gathered up her handbag and a sweater.

"That's right," Hillary said, "but there's something you should know."

Jane felt a twinge of alarm. "I was afraid of this. What?"

"Get in the car. I'll tell you while we drive."

Hillary backed out of the driveway without looking, and Jane closed her eyes, hoping there were no cars coming up the street. The screech of brakes told her there had been, but she kept her eyes closed, nevertheless. There were times when that was the only way to ride comfortably with Hillary at the wheel.

"OK," Hillary said, "this is a birthday party and family reunion we're planning." The big Cadillac lurched with the power of a frightened beast as she shifted from reverse to park.

"So far, so good," Jane said.

Hillary gunned the engine. "Why won't this car go?"

"Take it out of park, Hillary."

Hillary moved the lever, and the car lurched again.

"The honoree is America Elizabeth Bean. You know who Cassandra Bean is, don't you? That's her great aunt."

"Uh-huh."

"Open your eyes, Jane, this is important."

Jane opened her eyes with caution and glanced at Hillary.

"Well?" Hillary looked at Jane with an unexplained air of expectancy.

"Well what?"

A car at the intersection in front of them had to swerve off the street when Hillary ran a stop sign she apparently didn't see because her eyes were still on Jane. "Don't you *know* about America Elizabeth Bean?"

"Never heard of her."

There was a pause during which Hillary actually moved her eyes back to the street. "This is not going to be an ordinary party." She spoke without looking at Jane.

"Nothing you do is ever ordinary, Hillary, and I wouldn't expect anyone related to Cassandra Bean to be ordinary, either." Jane glanced at Hillary. Her silence was beginning to make Jane nervous. "Are you going to tell me about this America Elizabeth? I mean, what is it about her that makes her so different?"

"She—uh, well, she's been dead for several years. I don't know, four or five, maybe."

Jane's eyes widened. "Wait a minute. Let me get this

straight. This is a birthday party for a woman who's dead? For maybe five years?''

"Did I say birthday party? Hillary gave Jane a benign smile. "It's really just a party in her honor. Although it happens to be on her birthday.''

"Well . . .'' Jane gave a little shrug. "I guess that's not too unusual. I mean, we celebrate Lincoln's birthday and Washington's. Martin Luther King. Jesus Christ. She must have been some kind of family matriarch or something.''

"Oh yes, she was. You might say she was something of a hero. Or is that heroine? Anyway, it all started after she killed that woman, and I'm so glad you're being understanding and open about this, Jane. I think you're really going to enjoy this because the Beans are such interesting—''

"Hold on a minute. Hold on! You said she did what? Killed a woman?''

"Well, yes, sort of.''

"What do you mean, sort of? You either kill someone or you don't.''

"What I mean is, some people said she was already dead anyway.''

"What?!'' Jane turned away from Hillary a moment, looking out the window, trying to regain some semblance of balance. They had reached the edge of town now, and there was nothing to see except a forest of pine and cypress, so dense and tangled it was dark and becoming darker under the cloud-blackened sky. "This is getting too weird, Hillary.''

"I can explain.''

"I hope so.''

"It's simple, really, because the woman she killed was um . . . she was . . . a ghost.''

"A ghost! Oh, yes, that explains it.''

"I've known you long enough that I can tell when you're being sarcastic, Jane. This woman that America killed, her name was Virginia Blaylock, and she was a distant relative who was dead at the time.'' Hillary's right hand fluttered off the steering wheel as she spoke. "By that, I mean, she had a tombstone and people had seen her in her coffin. But then she started haunting people, including America Elizabeth, and so she killed her. And there was . . .'' She took both her hands off the wheel to make a shrugging gesture. ''Well, there was a body again, so they buried her again, and everybody was glad because she'd been trying to get the Beans off of the land she had said was hers.''

''Uh-huh.''

''That sounded sarcastic, Jane.''

''Put your eyes back on the road, Hillary, there's a truck coming around that curve.''

Hillary turned her attention back to the road. There was a long, uneasy silence between them until Hillary passed the truck and took her eyes off the road again and spoke to Jane. ''Aren't you going to say anything?''

''What is there to say? You're right, it's all so simple and ordinary. A party for a woman who's been dead five years. She's being honored because she killed someone who was already dead. I mean, what could be simpler?'' Jane turned suddenly toward Hillary again. ''She's not going to be there, is she? America Elizabeth?''

''I just hate it when you get sarcastic.''

''Well, is she?''

''No, of course not. And it's not to honor her for killing someone, you understand. It's just to honor her life.''

''They're honoring the life of a murderess? I don't think I like this family.''

''I didn't say she was a murderer. It could have been self-defense,'' Hillary said, sounding defensive herself.

''But you don't know that!''

''I always assume the best is true.''

''Hillary, you shouldn't just *assume* everything. You should check these things out.''

''Jane, Jane, Jane! You worry too much. Everything will be fine.'' She waved her hand again. ''Now! Let's talk about the theme for the party. Something festive, don't you think? We should use lots of light—candles of course— and flowers. The meal, I think, can be hearty this time of year. Stuffed millet balls to start it off, and then maybe either a crown roast or Cornish game hens. We'll need a salad, certainly. Maybe cabbage seasoned with amaranth. I'll need you to help me find the tablecloths—something cheerful. We'll have to brainstorm that. And the candles. Look for tapers in . . . What? White? I don't know. What do you think, Jane?''

Hillary continued her planning through lunch at a small diner. (She was appalled at the salad made of iceberg lettuce.) She was still chattering about the party when they stopped for gas at a station off the main highway. Before Jane could get out of the car to pump the gas, a youngish man came out of the station to Hillary's window.

"Premium or regular?" He had a nice smile with very white teeth and hazel eyes. A shock of brown hair fell across his forehead, giving him a boyish look.

"Premium, of course," Hillary said.

While the man filled her tank and cleaned her windshield, Hillary studied a map she'd brought along.

When the friendly young man took Hillary's credit card, he leaned forward and asked, "Can I help you find some place?"

"The Beans?" Hillary pointed to the map with the tip of her perfect mauve nail. "I thought there was supposed to be a road going east here."

Jane noticed that the man's face had grown suddenly pale, and he dropped the wet cloth he'd used on the windshield onto his lizard-skin boots.

"Beans? Never heard of a family by that name." He snatched Hillary's credit card and hurried into the building. When he returned with her receipt, he handed it to her without a word and seemed to be in a hurry to get back into the building.

"Full service just isn't what it used to be," Hillary said. She started the car and pulled away, narrowly missing the gas pump. As they drove, the forest became more and more dense and tangled, but they at last found a narrow, unpaved road on which they could turn east.

The road took them deeper and deeper into a shadowy world, following a creek until they came upon a wooden bridge spanning the water, which now ran through a deep

ravine. A half mile beyond the bridge was a house turned
gray from lack of paint. It rose to three stories and wore
the shadows of the surrounding trees like a dark cloak. The
wind that came with the clouds moved the tree branches in
a slow, ominous dance. A high stone fence rose around a
small plot a few feet from the house. When they got close
enough to the iron gate, they could see that the plot was a
graveyard, with some of the headstones fallen to the
ground.

"Cheerful looking place," Jane said as she and Hillary
got out of the car. A spattering of rain started just as they
reached the front entrance. They both saw, in the same
instant, the black wreath that hung there.

"Is this the Bean's idea of decor for the party?" Jane
asked, nodding toward the wreath.

"I don't know," Hillary said. She reached for the brass
knocker, but before she could grasp it, the door opened. A
small, ancient woman stood before them. Hillary started to
speak. "Hello, I'm here to see Cassandra Bean about—"

"Cassandra? Why, she's dead," the woman said before
Hillary could say another word.

2

"Cassandra can't be dead. That's impossible! She hired me to plan a birthday party." Hillary was bending over the tiny woman as if she were about to devour her.

The woman held the door open. "You'd best come in."

Hillary stepped inside, and Jane followed, eager to get out of the rain, which was falling harder now. Hillary was still agitated. "This certainly wasn't in the contract."

"I'm sorry to hear about your loss," Jane said, looking around the large, gaping entry hall. She was standing behind Hillary and trying to make amends for what seemed to her to be Hillary's lack of manners. "You're in no mood to talk about a party now, I'm sure, so maybe we'll just leave and—"

"Oh, there'll be a party, dearie." The old woman cackled.

Jane persisted. "But someone in your family has just died, I'm sure you won't be up to—"

The woman's rheumy old eyes caught fire as they bored into Jane. "Cassie always loved a party. This is the way she would have wanted it." The old woman spoke with gravity, but there was a passion seething somewhere that gave her pronouncement the sound of an angry prophet dispensing the word of God. As if she had ordered the theatrics, a loud clap of thunder shouted its amen. The old woman moved away with her stooped, shuffling walk toward two heavy wooden doors leading off the hall to the right. She passed through them without a look back, obviously taking for granted that Hillary and Jane would follow.

Behind the old woman's back, Jane gave Hillary a raised-eyebrow look. Hillary shrugged in response, but they both followed the woman into a room filled with the ponderous dark furniture of another century. The room appeared meticulously clean, yet a film of gloom clung to everything: the furniture, the fringed cloths that draped the tables and sofas, the heavy, faded forest green velvet drapes hanging from arched windows. Just below the high, embossed ceiling hung a row of trophy heads. The dead animals' glassy eyes shone with a grotesque brightness in the dusky room.

The woman turned to face them. "Wait here. She'll be with you soon." She moved toward another set of doors at the end of the room and disappeared.

Jane turned immediately to Hillary. "Who'll be with us? She didn't mean Cassandra, did she?"

"Well, of course not. She must mean whoever is going to take over now that Cassandra is . . . is no longer in charge." Long silver nails of rain pounded on the roof and tried to drive themselves through the window. Hillary glanced around at the room. "You know, this room could really be spectacular if we got rid of the drapes and use the natural light from those windows." She glanced around her. "I think I'd use a pale yellow carpet and white pine—"

"This place is really scary, Hillary."

"But a yellow carpet would do wonders, and—"

"I'm not talking about the carpet, for Christ's sake. I'm talking about the whole atmosphere of the place. That old woman, for instance. She looks like the housekeeper from *Rebecca*. You know, where the innocent young heroine gets trapped in the dark old house. And the way she talked! Like some character Woody Allen would dream up on a bad day. And this storm! I swear, it would be funny if it wasn't so

creepy.'' Jane glanced over her shoulder. ''Those dead eyes
up there on those poor unfortunate moose or reindeer or
whatever they are just make my skin crawl.''

''We just have to make the best of it, Jane.''

''Make the best of it? Everybody's *dead.* The honoree,
the hostess. Kinda makes you wonder who's next, doesn't
it?''

''Don't be so negative, Jane. Not everyone is dead, and
anyway, it's not so unusual to try to go ahead with life in
the face of loss or a tragedy. I'm sure we'll find everyone
here is ordinary.''

''So sorry to have kept you waiting.'' The voice was
loud, the Southern accent thick.

Jane and Hillary turned in unison toward the doors at the
end of the room where the old woman had exited. Jane's
breath caught in her throat at what she saw. A very large
woman in a brilliant, multicolored caftan of mostly red,
purple, and orange moved toward them. Her hair formed a
wide, wiry halo around her head and was died the same
electric orange as the swirls in her caftan. She carried a
huge gray cat in her arms. The cat screeched and jumped
out of her arms as soon as it saw Hillary and Jane.

''I'm Lotus Bean.'' The hand the woman extended toward Jane was as multicolored as her caftan, but along with
the brilliant colors were streaks of white and ochre as well.
Looking down at her hand, Lotus laughed. ''Oh, forgive
me. I've been painting, and I didn't take the time to wash
up once I realized how long I'd kept y'all waiting. I was
just so engrossed, you see, on getting it right. I was having
trouble with the shadows. You know, under the eyes? They
have to be just right. The life of the painting is in the shadows.'' Lotus rubbed her hands down the sides of her caftan.
''You're here to talk about the party. Cassie's party for
America Elizabeth.''

''Yes, I'm Hillary Scarborough. I've been hired to do the
planning and catering, but I imagine you'll want to cancel
in light of—''

Lotus's plump face crumpled. ''Poor Cassie! We never
got along, but she *was* kin.'' She pulled a handkerchief

from somewhere in her sleeve and dabbed at her eyes.

The cat was staring at Jane, hunched in a position to pounce.

"Interesting animal," Jane said.

Lotus glanced down at the cat. "Hieronymus! Naughty girl," she said while she dabbed at her eyes.

"Look," Jane said. "I'm sure, under the circumstances, you won't want to have the party, but we can reschedule later when—"

"Oh, but the party *has* to go on. Cassie wants it that way." Lotus tucked the tissue she'd been using into her bosom, and she seemed to tuck away her grief as well. "Now, about the party . . ." Her voice was as bright as her hair. "I think the weather will be a little bit too damp for anything outdoorsy, but I thought we could clear out the—"

Jane placed a hand on Lotus's arm. "You don't have to do this. I know you must have other things on your mind: the funeral, notifying relatives." Jane patted her arm. "Please don't feel pressured to throw a party."

Lotus glanced first at Hillary, then at Jane, as if she wasn't quite sure what she should do.

"You're right, Jane." Hillary said. She glanced at Lotus. "You must be in shock. After all, Cassandra was young, wasn't she? It must have come as a surprise."

"A surprise?" Lotus seemed distracted, but she recovered quickly. "Oh yes! I mean, well, murder is always a surprise, isn't it?"

Hillary brought one of her hands up to her mouth and in the process knocked a vase from the adjacent table. Crystal shards splattered like water droplets. Hieronymus screeched and fled from the room.

"Murder?" Jane said in the same instant as the crash. Lotus was looking at both of them, her eyes wide and both of her pudgy hands covering her mouth. It was hard to tell whether she was alarmed about the vase or if she was afraid more of her own words would escape. "Why?" Jane asked. "I mean, why would you say that, and why would anyone want to murder her?"

Lotus shook her head. "I didn't mean to say that. I shouldn't have said that."

Jane noticed the frightened look in her eyes. "Are you all right?"

"I'm not sure. I mean, yes. Yes, of course." She was pacing the floor, twisting the fabric at the end of her sleeve. "It seems sort of unreal to me. Just a kind of an illusion. You know what I mean? Like a watercolor when the light is—"

"Lotus, what makes you think she was murdered?" Jane asked again, exchanging a quick glance with Hillary.

"Murdered?" Lotus looked alarmed and a bit disoriented. "Oh dear, I shouldn't have said that." Twist, twist, went her hand on the sleeve. "You see, I'm just upset over Cassie passing at such a young age, and I say things I don't mean. People do that, you know—say things they don't mean when they're upset."

Jane frowned. "Has the sheriff been notified? You're awfully upset. Maybe you'd feel better if you talked to the sheriff."

"No, no. I couldn't possibly. This is a family matter. It's not something I could ever discuss with—"

Hillary, whose face was still uncommonly white, spoke again, but in a choked, frightened voice. "I'm sure she's right. This is none of our business. We'll just be going now, won't we?" She clutched her Dooney bag like a frightened child as she hurried toward the door.

"No, no. Wait a minute!" Jane took a few steps toward Hillary. "What? Are we all crazy here? Murder is not a simple little family affair."

"Jane, we don't even know for sure if it's—"

"Look, we have a responsibility here." Jane turned to Lotus. "If you think someone was murdered, you have to call the sheriff."

Lotus glanced uneasily at the ancient telephone sitting on a table like a black vulture in a nest of coiled wire. Then, suddenly, she burst into tears. "Oh dear, I shouldn't be talking about this to you." She sobbed as she spoke. "Aunt Lizzie doesn't approve of—Oh dear!" She cried harder.

"And anyway who would believe me if I told the truth?" she said when she had gained some semblance of control again.

"There must be something, even if it's a subconscious thought, that made you say she was murdered," Jane said.

"Well, there was . . . a woman." Lotus wore a troubled look.

"A woman?" Hillary asked.

"I saw her coming out of Cassie's room just before . . ."

"Before?" Jane prodded.

"Just before Cousin, uh, Cousin Winston said Cassie was dead."

"The woman murdered her?" Hillary asked.

Lotus shook her head violently. "She wasn't murdered. That just slipped out because Cousin . . . Winston said . . . well, he said . . ."

"Yes, Lotus," Jane prompted.

"That it was her heart. And he was right, of course. It was her heart."

"Lotus, call the sheriff." Jane was emphatic. "Tell him about the woman you saw coming out of Cassandra's room. And listen to us; now is not the time to plan a party. You have to get this off your mind and get through the funeral. You're still in shock now. We can talk in a few weeks."

"She's right." Hillary said. "Here's my business card." She pulled it from her bag. "Give me a call in a few weeks. It's best to postpone. Of course we could redo this room before the party. You'd be surprised at how yellow carpet can affect depression."

"No, no, no!" Lotus shook her head and made her orange hair swirl in a violent storm. "You can't just leave and tell me to call the sheriff. You don't understand. I can't tell anyone who I saw."

"Why not?" Jane asked.

"Because it was a ghost."

"A ghost?" Jane was puzzled.

"You have *got* to get rid of this carpet and those dark drapes, too," Hillary said.

"And that's not all." Lotus's face was a white mask

beneath her neon hair, and she spoke in a low, frightened voice that was almost a whisper.

"I was afraid it wasn't." Hillary turned a quick, worried glance to Jane.

"It was someone I know. It was America Elizabeth, and she told me this would lead to death. More death, I mean."

"I see," Jane said gently. She had begun to doubt the sanity of the woman. "Maybe you should discuss this with your family. They'll help you decide what to do."

"Don't patronize me!" Lotus's words were surprisingly iced with anger. "I know what you're thinking. That I've gone around the bend. Well, I haven't! But I can't tell any of *them* about this. They'll all think I'm crazy, just like you two. Do you know what it's like living with five people who think you're insane? All of them: Aunt Julia and Uncle Bruce, Cousin Katrin and Aunt Lizzie—you met her in the hall—and Cousin Winston. Even Cassie thought I was touched in the head because I see things—things I wish I didn't see."

"Like ghosts walking the halls?" Jane tried to keep her voice soft and soothing.

Lotus answered in a whisper. "Yes. And things like Mandy Thornburg. I saw her drowning in that pool a week before it happened."

"Are you telling us you're psychic?" Jane asked.

"Of course," Lotus said. "And I can converse with the dead."

"We really have to go," Hillary said.

Lotus turned to her. "Oh, you'll never get out now. That little bridge just down the way. Something has happened to it."

Jane and Hillary both stared at her in silence.

"Go ahead." Lotus shooed them out with her hands. "See for yourself."

"OK," Jane said. "We're going, but if you're not going to talk to the sheriff about this, we'll make the call. I think it's only fair that I tell you that."

"Just go!" Lotus waved them out this time without looking at them.

Jane and Hillary hurried out of the room together. "I can't wait to get out of here," Jane whispered as they stepped into the vast, dark entry hall.

Aunt Lizzie, who had met them at the door, was nowhere to be seen now. It appeared they would have to let themselves out. Jane was just as anxious to leave as Hillary was, even more so as they moved toward the front exit and she saw someone watching them from behind a partially opened door on the left side of the hall.

Just as they opened the door, lightning flashed and thunder roared at them at almost the same instant. The rain had become a shroud, covering everything. Jane and Hillary were soaked by the time they reached the car.

"Whew!" Jane said, when they were safely enclosed in Hillary's big Cadillac. "I don't care what you say, Hillary, there's not enough yellow carpet in the entire universe to make that place cheerful."

Hillary started the car and backed into a small shrub.

"Maybe we overreacted. Maybe there's a perfectly normal explanation for—"

"For what? Somebody who talks to the dead? You're *not* still thinking of doing that job, are you?"

"Well . . ." Part of the shrub had become stuck in the underbelly of the car and was now making a scraping noise as they drove out of the driveway.

"Hillary!"

"I know they're a little odd, but I can't help wondering if I ought to turn down a client."

"You're changing your mind? You actually want to go back in there?"

"A client means money, you know."

"How do you know it means money? They're a bunch of crazies in that house. They'll probably pay you with Monopoly money. And besides, just a moment ago, you were as anxious to get out of there as I was."

"OK, I'll admit I was a little taken aback there for a minute, but when you think about it, who's to say what crazy really is?"

"I'll tell you what crazy really is. Back there, in that house. That's what crazy really is. Forget about the money, Hillary, and think about what we just saw. Do you really want to go back to that place? Do you really want those dead animal eyes staring down at you? Do you really want to hear someone with multicolored hands channel the dead?"

"Well, when you put it that way . . ."

"There'll be other parties to cater, other houses to decorate. Just take my word for it, you're better off."

"You're probably right."

"I know I'm right. Now, where's your cell phone?"

"Are you really going to call the sheriff?"

"Of course I am. If there's been a murder, someone has to report it."

"But she kept denying it."

"And that makes it all the more suspicious. Hillary, we'd be remiss if we didn't tell the authorities about this."

"Well, all right, but I'm telling you, Jane, I don't want to get mixed up in anything that's, well, messy. You got me involved in that business of a dead woman you found in that house we were going to redecorate a few months ago."

"What do you mean, *I* got *you* involved? It was you who . . . Oh, never mind. Where's your phone?"

"In my bag." Hillary was uncharacteristically preoccupied with her driving; the road was becoming slick from the rain, and the wipers were doing a frenetic repetitious dance across the windshield.

Jane pulled the phone out of Hillary's bag and turned it on. The phone beeped, flashed a signal, then went dead. "What's wrong with this phone?"

Hillary reached for the phone, then took her other hand off the steering wheel to press the power button. "Oh dear, the battery's dead."

"Hillary! The road!"

Hillary turned her eyes back to the road, then suddenly

applied the brakes when she saw what Jane had seen. The road had disappeared, swallowed by a deep ravine that was now filling with water. The remnants of the bridge dangled from a broken timber.

3

Hillary jerked the Cadillac into reverse and stomped on the accelerator without looking back. The car lurched, throwing Jane's head first forward and then back against the headrest. The big car swerved to the left on the slippery, muddy road and failed to respond to Hillary's frantic twisting of the steering wheel.

There was a thump. Jane turned around quickly to see a young pine tree swaying from the blow Hillary had given its trunk.

Hillary pressed the accelerator all the way to the floor, making the motor growl and scream. "Oh dear, I think we're stuck!"

"You still have it in reverse, Hillary! Put it in drive before you knock that tree down on us!"

"Oh, silly me." She shifted into drive and gunned the engine again. The tires went into a futile spin for a few seconds until they caught hold and the car lurched forward, toward the ravine. Hillary jerked the wheel and they swerved again. The car spun, turning them around one hundred eighty degrees.

Jane looked back and got a sick feeling when she saw the rear end of the car actually hanging over the edge of the ravine the broken bridge had once spanned.

In spite of the noise of the rain on the roof of the car, Jane could hear great globs of mud breaking off the edge of the ravine and falling into the water below.

Hillary, for once, was speechless. She looked at Jane, a question in her eyes.

"Give it the gas!" Jane said, gambling that the tires could get enough purchase to propel them forward.

Hillary's chic brown pump went down hard on the accelerator. The Cadillac seemed to crouch in the mud, then the tires took hold on what little firm ground was left. The big car spun away from the edge and was once again on the muddy road leading back to the Beans'.

"Can you believe that?" Hillary was twisting the steering wheel erratically, trying to keep the car from skidding more on the mud while in reality she was making it worse. "I mean, it's amazing. How did that woman know the bridge was out? Do you think she's really psychic? Is something wrong, Jane? You don't look like you feel well."

"Do . . . do you want me to drive?"

"Now, why ever would I want to do that? If we changed drivers now, we'd both get wet."

"The road, Hillary. Watch the road."

"Well, I don't know why. The only place it goes is back to the Beans'. It's not like we have a choice or anything."

When they had left the decrepit old house a few minutes earlier, Jane would never have believed she would be so happy to see it again. At least they wouldn't have to drive any farther.

Hillary stopped the car and turned to Jane. "Now what do we do?"

"We either stay here in the car until somebody rebuilds the bridge, which may take days, or we go back inside."

Hillary simply looked at her without speaking. Jane sensed that Hillary was as reluctant as she was to go back into the old house with its weird occupants, in spite of her earlier talk about the value of a client.

"OK." Hillary sounded reluctant but resigned.

"OK," Jane said. They each opened a door and raced out into the torrent. They were both dripping as they reached the front entrance of the house and stood hunched against the dampness as they waited for someone to respond to their knock.

Finally, the door opened, and the same old woman who had greeted them earlier stood before them. She raised her rheumy eyes to glance at them briefly, then lowered them again and stepped aside, speaking in her creaky voice. "I have your rooms ready."

Jane and Hillary exchanged glances, then stepped inside. The old woman quickly disappeared through one of the doors leading off the entry hall. The storm had obviously knocked out the electricity, so the hall was dimly lit by candles that dripped from sconces high on the wall, sending black smoke up to the curved ceiling, which was molded in designs resembling all manner of fruits as well as cherubs trailing ribbons. The flickering candlelight made shadows dance along the walls while an eerie yellow light spilled out of the wide opening that led to the library where, Jane remembered, the heads of dead animals hung.

"What's that supposed to mean?" Hillary asked. "How did she know we would be back?"

"I told her." The loud voice boomed from somewhere unseen, and then in the next moment, Lotus appeared in the yellow light of the library's open doorway, her mass of frizzy orange hair encircling her head in an even wilder fashion, as if some of the electricity from the storm outside had trapped itself there. Her caftan rippled around her flesh like ocean waves as she moved. "You didn't believe me when I told you I see things, did you? I saw the bridge. I saw you coming back."

"The bridge washes out often, does it?" Jane asked.

Lotus gave her a knowing look. "You think it was just conjecture on my part. A storm, a bridge, a one-way road so you'd have to turn around." She shrugged. "Call it logic if you like. Call it anything you want, but I can tell you this: That bridge hasn't washed out in fifteen years."

"Oh my!" Hillary was wide-eyed.

"Could I use the phone?" Jane asked. She was trying to squeeze herself through the doorway to the library, which Lotus was blocking with her massive body.

"The phone's dead," Lotus said. "The storm must have knocked it out."

Jane lifted the receiver and put it to her ear. There was no dial tone, nothing except dead silence. She put the receiver down with a sigh.

Lotus moved toward the stairs, then turned back to motion to Jane and Hillary. "Follow me. I'll show you to your rooms, and you can get out of those wet clothes." She sized each of them up with her eyes. "Cassie has some things that will fit each of you, and I don't suppose she'll be needing them for a while." Lotus started up the dark stairway, then turned around again after she'd gone a few steps. "Come on!" She sounded impatient. "You want to catch your death?"

"Wait a minute!" Hillary's voice was urgent, and she grabbed Jane's arm as if for support. "What do you mean by 'for a while'? I mean, if she's dead, she's not going to be walking around looking for her clothes, is she?"

Lotus made a dismissive wave with her hand as she spoke over her shoulder. "You just never know, in this house. I mean, it's not like she'd be the first ghost to walk around in here. I've already told you about America Elizabeth." She turned back again, looking down at Jane and Hillary, who still hadn't moved from the foot of the stairs. "Are you coming or not?"

Hillary's hand tightened on Jane's arm as she looked at Jane, eyes wide.

Jane lifted a soggy strand of hair away from her eyes and gave a little shrug. "She's right. We ought to at least get out of these wet clothes."

Hillary kept her hand locked on Jane's arm as they climbed the stairs. Lotus stopped at the top of the landing and pointed down the hall. Candles mounted in sconces cast small splotches of yellow light into the length of the hall, and the flickering made shadows waltz on the walls and ceiling.

"There, that first room on the left." Lotus pointed, allowing the wide sleeve of her caftan to sweep outward in a dramatic movement. "That's your room, Jane. And Hillary, yours is the third." She turned around to start down the stairs but turned around again to face them. "Oh, and don't go into that room in between your two rooms. Dinner is at five. The dining room is the second door to the left off the entry hall." She moved away, hurrying down the hall.

"Wait a minute!" Jane took a quick step toward her. Lotus turned back to her with an impatient look. "We really weren't planning on spending the night or anything," Jane continued. "I mean, if you can just loan us something dry to wear, we'll be on our way and send it back to—"

"Where do you propose to go?" Lotus still had her impatient look.

"Well, I'm sure there must be another way out of here." Jane was speaking too fast, running her words together in a nervous way, but Lotus's attitude was making her uneasy. "I mean, I'm sure it will probably take a little longer, but we really don't mind as long as we—"

Lotus's eyes grew cold. "There's not another way out of here. You're stuck here. Just like the rest of us have been for years."

"What? What do you mean, for years?" There was no answer to Jane's question as Lotus turned away again and floated down the stairs, caftan billowing in the shadows of the stairwell. Jane turned back with a sigh to see Hillary standing, dripping, in the dark hallway, her eyes wide with fright.

"What have you gotten us into, Jane?"

"Me? What are you talking about? It was you who took this job. It was you who, just a few minutes ago, was talking about how you couldn't pass up paying clients."

"Jane! You're always getting into legal nuances like that, just because you've had two semesters of law school. And now is not the time for it!" Hillary's voice was an urgent whisper.

Jane opened her mouth and pointed a finger at Hillary to

set her straight, but she'd known her long enough to realize it wouldn't do any good. She dropped her finger, took a deep breath, and said, "You're right, Hillary. Now is not the time for it. Let's both get out of these wet clothes. Then we'll meet in my room and decide what to do."

"Good idea." Hillary turned to open her door.

"Oh, and Hillary. It was two years of law school. Not two semesters."

"Whatever."

Jane opened her own door and stepped inside. An oil lamp on a bedside table had been lit, throwing more light than there had been in the hallway. A dress made of some soft black material that could have been rayon or silk had been laid out on the bed. It was a simple A-line design with long sleeves, a flared, ankle-length skirt, and a scooped neckline; a classic black dress, Jane thought, that could be made to look formal or casual. Beside it on the bed was a pair of soft slippers in black and gold.

A pitcher of water sitting inside a crockery bowl was on the dry sink, and next to the water was a bar of soap and a large Turkish towel. The whole room had been set up as if Jane had been expected all along. It gave her an eerie feeling, but she shook it off and indulged herself with the warm water and soap, then dried herself, including her hair, with the big towel. She slipped on the dress and slippers. The shoes pinched a little, and the dress was slightly too big in the waist, but at least they were dry. She used the lipstick she carried in her purse and had managed to make herself presentable by the time Hillary knocked at her door.

Hillary was dressed in hunter green, which accented the green of her eyes and was a perfect complement to the red glints in her auburn hair, which was still damp. The dress she wore fit her at least reasonably well. Both dresses were surprisingly chic and with a hint of formality as if that was what would be expected at dinner.

Hillary closed the door behind her and leaned against it. She uttered one word, which was almost a gasp. "Jane!" It was only then that Jane noticed how pale she looked.

"Is something wrong, Hillary?"

"That room next door. The one she told us not to go into?"

"Yes?"

"Cassandra's in there."

"What!"

"I mean, I think she's in there. There's a casket."

"A casket?"

"Yes. Right in the middle of the floor. The bed's been taken out to make room for it."

"Are you sure it wasn't something else?"

"Like what? I mean, what else looks like a casket?"

"I don't know, maybe . . ."

"It's a casket, Jane."

"The electricity is out, so it must have been dark in there. Maybe your eyes were playing tricks or—"

"There's somebody lying in it. I saw her. The head, the outline of her face."

"Right next door to us?"

"Right next door."

"Oh my God."

"We've got to get out of here, Jane."

"How?"

Hillary paced the room nervously. "You'll figure something out, won't you? I mean, you have to. After all, you're the smart one. You with your law degree. And besides that, California people are, well, so much more *experienced*."

"Stop pacing, Hillary, you're making me nervous. And I don't have a law degree. I only have two years of law school, and people from California are experienced in what? Walking on water? We can't get across that creek without a bridge."

"You don't expect me to spend the night next door to a dead woman, do you?"

"I don't see that we have any other choice."

"Come on now, hon, you've never let me down before."

"Hillary, don't get your hopes up. It may take days to repair that bridge."

"I don't pay you to be negative, Jane."

"You don't pay me nearly enough for being stranded in

this house and having to deal with the Beans.''

Hillary opened her mouth as if to argue with her, but she didn't speak a word. Instead, she gave a long sigh and sat on the edge of the bed, a defeated look creeping over her face. Hillary's helplessness always stirred some protective, motherly instinct in Jane, in spite of the fact that Hillary was at least ten years her senior.

Jane walked to the bed and put a hand on Hillary's shoulder. ''Try not to worry about it, Hill. Maybe the phones will be working again soon, and we can call someone to come out and put up some kind of temporary bridge.''

Hillary looked up at her and smiled. ''I knew you'd think of something.''

''It's not a promise. It's just a maybe. In the meantime, we'll have to make to the best of it.'' She pointed to the old-fashioned wind-up clock that sat on the bedside table. ''Look, it's almost five. Let's go see if we can find the dining room.''

Hillary stood up. ''OK, but first I want you to have a look in that room.''

''Don't you think that's being a little bit nosy? I mean, people shouldn't go snooping around in other people's houses.''

Hillary put her hands on her hips and gave Jane an impatient look. ''Jane Ferguson! You know you are just dying to see what's in there.''

''Well, maybe, but—''

''Come on. You have to see this.'' Hillary took her hand and pulled her toward the door. Jane gave in to her curiosity and let Hillary lead her out into the hall and up to the door of the room next to hers. ''It isn't locked,'' Hillary whispered as she grasped the old-fashioned cloisonné doorknob and pushed the door open a tiny crack. The hinges groaned, and Hillary stopped. She pushed again, and the groan and creak were even louder. Finally, a steady push brought a long, protracted moan from the hinges.

Hillary peered inside, then moved aside, pointing silently into the interior of the room. Jane leaned in front of her and peeked in. Just as Hillary had described, a casket sat in the middle of the floor, the top half opened, revealing a white quilted satin lining, and the young woman inside. Her long brown hair was spread out on a satin pillow. Her pale face in profile, except for the closed eyes, was exactly the same as the half-column picture that always ran in the newspaper with her weekly horoscope.

Suddenly, they heard the sound of voices. Jane pulled back, and Hillary closed the door quickly. They both cringed at the loud cry of the hinges; then they stood looking at each other, wide-eyed and frightened. Jane relaxed a little when she realized that the voices were coming from downstairs, as if there were people in the entry hall. Nevertheless, she grabbed Hillary's hand and pulled her away from the door.

"See what I mean?" Hillary's voice was an excited whisper.

"Yes, yes, I saw," Jane said, also whispering. "But what's so unusual about that? Isn't that sort of a Southern custom? For people to have the deceased in the home for a wake or something?" In spite of her rationalizing, she sounded anything but calm.

"Maybe. I mean it used to be more common than it is now. But it's still creepy. We have just got to get out of here!"

"I know! I know!" Jane was having a difficult time controlling her own panic. "Let's go have dinner. Maybe we'll both feel better. Then we'll meet in my room and talk about it."

Jane held Hillary's hand as they walked through the shadowy hall and down the darkened stairway. When they reached the entry hall, there was no longer anyone there. However, the second door on the left, which Lotus had told them led to the dining room, was open, with the glow of an oil lamp spilling out into the hall. When they stepped inside, the same yellow light made shadows on the ceiling like stalactites ready to form.

The low murmur that emanated from the five souls who sat around the long, dark slab of a table stopped; some with a fork halfway to the mouth, others with jaws paused in the process of chewing, all stared at the two of them.

"Oh!" said a tiny man with thinning gray hair and wire-rimmed glasses. "These must be the guests Lotus told us about. The ones who are going to do the party for America Elizabeth." Seated at the end of the table, he stood up to greet them. He seemed to slither around like a fish in a suit that was several sizes too big.

"Yes, Uncle Bruce, this is Jane and Hillary." Lotus pointed to them with a sweep of her pudgy arm. She was now wearing a short-sleeved, silky outfit of a gaudy orange that was exactly the color of her hair.

"America Elizabeth just loves a party, you know. She always looks forward to it every year," said a smiling woman who was seated next to Uncle Bruce. Her graying hair had come out of its pinned-up do and was curling around her face, giving her a look of careless good humor. A cameo brooch was pinned crookedly at the neckline of her faded lavender dress.

"Aunt Julia," Lotus said, pointing to the woman who had just spoken. "And that's Cousin Winston and Cousin Katrin." She indicated the young woman who sat next to Julia and the man across from her. Winston, who looked to be in his early forties, had hair that was like dark wild grass tinged with frost. It was combed back in an unruly pompadour to reveal a cushion of a face with features quilted into the folds. It was the face of someone who had lived hard and fast. His mouth twitched in a manner that might have been a smile, and he made a halfhearted gesture of rising slightly from his seat, but his glance moved quickly from Jane and Hillary to Julia.

"Now, Aunt Julia," his tone was sanguine, "you know America Elizabeth doesn't *always* appreciate what we do, and I have a feeling this year is going to be one of those times."

Katrin did not speak at all. She merely ducked her head, letting a curtain of hair droop forward to partially cover her plain face while she toyed with the food on her plate. Her long, thin fingers wrapped around the fork.

"Oh pooh!" said Julia with a wave of her hand. "You're

always too hard on her, dear. The younger generation can be so cynical.''

Bruce made a little fanfare toward the chair he was holding for Jane, and when she was seated, he hurried around the table in quick little steps to pull out a chair for Hillary, his suit undulating around him.

When they were seated, a door opened, and the woman Lotus had called Aunt Lizzie stepped into the room carrying two plates of food. She placed one each in front of Hillary and Jane, then slid into a chair at the end of the table opposite Bruce and attacked the leg and thigh of chicken on her plate.

''No matter how gay the party, it just won't be the same without Cassie,'' Julia said.

Katrin looked up for the first time and spoke. ''I can't imagine that you would care, Aunt Julia. She treated you as if you were an idiot.''

''Oh now, Katrin,'' Julia said, but Katrin was hiding behind her hair again.

''Cassie's spirit is still around, dearie, so it'll be just the same,'' Aunt Lizzie said without looking up from her plate.

''True, true,'' Winston said with a nod of his head.

''It's such a lovely thing for the two of you to do, helping Cassie plan the party,'' Julia said, glancing from Hillary to Jane.

Jane had been looking at the leg and thigh on her plate, thinking that they looked disturbingly like human body parts, but she glanced up quickly when Julia spoke to her. ''Well, I'm not sure we're going to be able to, you know, actually do it.''

''Oh! Why ever not?'' Julia looked as if she was about to cry.

''It's a family tradition!'' Lotus sounded as disturbed as Julia. ''We always have a party.''

''Of course, and someone must have planned it before we came along.'' Jane did her best to keep her voice light. She glanced at Hillary, hoping for some help, maybe some excuse for why they wouldn't be handling the job, but Hillary had turned her attention to Lizzie.

"You know, you can add roasted cherry tomatoes and onions to a dish like this and change it from plain to elegant." She leaned toward her and added, "And another little secret of mine is to serve it with couscous."

Lizzie turned toward her with an angry expression and used her fork to point to a plate of black mounds on a platter in the center of the table. "There's blood pudding if you want a side dish," she said.

"Oh—no, thank you," Hillary stammered. "Blood pudding goes with beef, not chicken."

Winston laughed. "In Aunt Lizzie's house, it goes with everything."

"You best stick to your bargain and plan the party, dearie." Lizzie was still staring at Hillary, ignoring Winston.

"Oh, well, I'd like to, of course, but Jane has a scheduling conflict, and I just can't do it without her, you know."

"Has to be special this year." There was a menacing tone to Lizzie's voice.

"Oh, I'm sure it does, and I would love to do it, but what can I say? Jane says no."

Jane visualized herself reaching across the table and choking Hillary. She didn't want crazy Lizzie mad at her for being the one who canceled the party.

"How do the two of you like your rooms?" Winston pointed at both Hillary and Jane with the chicken leg he was holding.

"Well, now that you mention it," Hillary said. "You wouldn't happen to have anything, say, on the first floor? You see, Jane has this condition that makes climbing stairs difficult, so if—"

"She seemed all right to me when we went up," Lotus said, "and besides, we don't have any bedrooms down here."

Julia leaned toward Jane. "Is it your heart, dear? America Elizabeth has a bad heart, too, you know."

Jane managed only a weak smile in response to Julia. She cut off a piece of the chicken, silently hoping the bizarre meal would be over soon. She could only be grateful that the meal was simple and not a protracted seven or eight courses. It was over after the rhubarb pie.

She and Hillary both declined the family's invitation to join them in the drawing room, pleading exhaustion. "But I would like to try the telephone again, just in case it's been restored," Jane said.

"It hasn't been," Lotus said in a bored, tired voice.

Jane didn't dare ask how she knew that, but when she and Hillary left the dining room, she whispered to Hillary, "You go on upstairs and wait for me. I'll slip into the library and try the phone."

"Go upstairs? By myself?" They were speaking in whispers again.

"Go on, Hillary. I'll be right there. As soon as my heart condition will allow it, at least."

"Now, Jane, don't be mad at me. I had to think of something."

"Just go, Hillary. I want them to hear you climbing the stairs so they'll think we're both up there. I want to find out if they're lying to us about the phones."

"But why would they do that?"

"Who knows why. We just had dinner with the Addams Family. They could be up to just about anything."

"Well, all right," Hillary said, her forehead creased with a worried frown. "Just hurry."

Jane did hurry as much as was possible. She slipped into the library and went to the table where the ancient telephone rested, hoping for the best, but when she placed the heavy receiver to her ear, there was only dead silence. There was no way of knowing how long they'd be stuck in the Bean house.

She walked up the stairs as quietly as possible, dreading to tell Hillary. She was surprised to see Hillary waiting for her on the landing.

"What are you doing?" Jane asked. "I told you to meet me in my room."

"We've got to get out of here, Jane."

"I know, I know. We will as soon as we can, but I'm afraid I've got some bad news."

''No, I've got some bad news.''

''What?''

Hillary pointed down the hall toward their rooms. ''It's Cassandra. She's not in her casket.''

4

"Not in her casket? Oh, come on, Hillary."

"No, I mean it." Hillary still sounded scared. "Have a look for yourself." She took Jane's hand and led her down the hall. When they reached the door leading into Cassandra's room, she stopped and turned to Jane, her face white. "There is something very wrong going on here." She spoke in a hushed tone. "I knew it as soon as we drove up to this place and I saw those rose bushes."

"Rose bushes?"

Hillary nodded emphatically. "They should have been pruned weeks ago."

Jane rolled her eyes. "Oh sure. I always say, anyone who forgets to prune rose bushes is sure to be up to no good."

"For heaven's sake, Jane, don't make light of this." She spoke in a hoarse voice as she pointed a trembling, mauve-tipped finger at the door. "There's no one in that casket!"

Jane glanced at the closed door, then spoke in the hushed tones one might use in a funeral parlor. "How could you see the casket with the door closed? You didn't open it again, did you?"

"Well, not exactly, but sort of."

"What does that mean?"

Hillary looked, for a moment, like a child caught disobeying. "I was on my way to my room, and I noticed that the door was open slightly, so I pushed it just the tiniest little bit, and it swung open."

Jane crossed her arms. "Amazing. And you looked inside, of course."

"Wouldn't you?"

"And then you closed it again."

Hillary gave her an indignant look. "Absolutely! I mean, what if she's in there? We don't want her out walking around the halls, do we?"

"Hillary, have you gone completely around the bend?"

"You don't believe me, do you? Go on, have a look for yourself."

Jane hesitated only a moment, placed her hand on the doorknob and turned it, opening the door slowly, her eyes still on Hillary. She glanced inside at the casket with the lamp still burning beside it and felt her heart skip a beat. She closed the door and looked at Hillary again. When she was finally able to speak, the only words she could utter were, "Oh my God!"

"You see what I mean, Jane? We've got to get out of here."

Jane nodded, but some perverse urge compelled her to open the door again and look inside at the empty casket. She reclosed the door to Cassandra's room as quietly as possible, took a deep breath, and turned back to Hillary. "There's got to be some logical explanation for this."

Hillary grabbed her arm in an urgent manner. "I don't care what the explanation is, I don't want to stay here a minute longer."

"We've got to stay calm, Hillary," Jane said. "Come into my room, and let's talk about this."

Hillary followed Jane so closely that she bumped into her when Jane paused to open the door to her room. Once inside, Hillary scurried to the closet, took a cautious look within, then moved on to the heavy, green drapes and peered behind them. She stooped to glance under the bed, then straightened and turned. "I think we're alone."

"Of course we are. Why wouldn't we be?"

"Well, she's got to be somewhere, doesn't she?"

"You're right about that." Jane sat on the edge of the bed, her brow wrinkled in a frown. She bit her bottom lip. "Like I said, there has to be a logical explanation."

Hillary gave her a worried look. "Maybe we should talk to Lotus about this. Or maybe that Winston person. Or Uncle Bruce."

Jane gave a wry little laugh. "I have a feeling they'd all think it was perfectly normal. I mean, they all talk about that dead woman they call America Elizabeth as if she were still alive. They just seem to take for granted that she's a ghost and that she has the run of the house."

"Oh Lord, that means there are two ghosts roaming around."

"Hillary, you're beginning to sound as crazy as everyone else in this loony bin. You know there's no such thing as ghosts. If Cassandra is not in that casket, then she's not really dead, or someone removed the body."

"But if she's not dead, why was she in the casket to begin with?" Hillary asked.

Before Jane could answer, lightning danced across the sky, accompanied by an exploding drumroll of thunder. Jane saw Hillary glance at the window as the storm's display lit up the sky, then her eyes grew wide. "Jane, look!"

Jane looked toward the window, but all she could see was darkness and the droplets of rain on the pane. "What is it, Hillary?"

"Over there, where the house makes an L, there's a little balcony."

Jane leaned closer to the window. "So?"

"There's someone out there," Hillary whispered.

"In this rain?"

Hillary nodded. "I think it's Cassandra's ghost."

"You know, Hillary, I'm really beginning to worry about you." Lightning tore another rip in the sky, and this time Jane saw the woman on the balcony. The wind tangled her long hair around her face, and she was dressed in what could have been a shroud. She did, indeed, look like Cassandra.

"Did you see that? It's her, isn't it?" Hillary sounded excited.

"Well, if it is, it's no ghost you're seeing." In spite of her show of confidence, an eerie sensation crawled up Jane's spine.

"You mean . . ."

"I mean a real live flesh-and-blood Cassandra."

"But why—"

I don't know. The mystery is why everyone in this family is pretending she's dead if she's up walking around." She glanced toward the door. "I wish that damned phone worked."

"That means you weren't able to talk to the sheriff?" Hillary stood, paced the floor. "I can't do this, Jane. I can't spend the night alone in that room, ghost or no ghost. Why, I won't get a minute's sleep."

"Hillary—"

"I mean, it's got that flowered wallpaper and a *plaid* bedspread. The rustic, eclectic look is all right, but it should be *coordinated.*

"You're worried about the wallpaper when we've got dead people walking around?" Jane regretted her words, chastising herself for not letting well enough alone.

Hillary's eyes widened. "So you admit it. There *are* dead people walking—"

"Forget it, Hillary. I didn't mean it. You're right. We should worry about the wallpaper."

Hillary gave a confident nod, then leaned toward Jane and spoke in a conspiratorial tone. "All of these rooms really are bad, you know." She straightened and threw her arms out. "Just look at this one. Those green velvet drapes. Just like the ones in the library. They look like they came out of Tara after it was ravaged by the Yankees. And that faded bedspread . . . Cassandra's room is just as bad. Who can blame her? I mean, it really is enough to wake the dead."

"Now, *there's* the old Hillary."

"I could do so much with just a few simple touches. You know, unbleached muslin curtains, a duvet cover in the same fabric for a down-filled comforter to replace the bedspreads. It would actually enhance the rustic old furniture, and then we could—"

"Go on, Hillary." You could always depend on Hillary's short attention span to keep her from getting too worried, Jane thought.

"Couldn't I just stay in here with you tonight?"

"Why would you do that when there's a perfectly good bed in your room? And when you close your eyes you won't see the wallpaper *or* the plaid bedspread."

"It's not just the decor, and you know it, Jane. I'm just trying to get my mind off of being in a haunted house. Come on now, admit it. Aren't you at least just a little bit scared?"

"Of course not. What's to be scared of?"

Jane reassured Hillary until she finally was able to convince her to go to her own room. Hillary went, reluctantly, but Jane had to go with her and stay until she had finished her routine of checking the closet, under the plaid-covered bed, and behind the green, velvet drapes.

In spite of her efforts to reassure Hillary, and perhaps herself, when Jane was back in her own room, it was a little eerie to be alone. Shadows danced on the wall and ceiling, cast there by the flickering light from the oil lamp, and something—she convinced herself it was a draft—made the closet door swing slightly on its creaky hinges. The storm continued to vent its rage on the night, rending the sky with fire.

Jane sat on the edge of her bed, watching the closet door swing back and forth and listening to it creak. She shivered, not from cold, but from the memory of the woman on the balcony. Why was a woman who was supposed to be dead walking around in the storm?

She forced herself to undress and put on the long, white cotton nightgown Lotus had provided for her. She took a small flashlight from her purse and placed it on the bedside table in case she needed to find the bathroom during the night. Once she was in bed, she pulled the covers up to her chin and lay there for a long time on her back, her eyes open. Hillary was right, she thought, the place was too creepy to sleep.

Finally, though, weariness from the long day won over her fears, and she dozed. She had no idea how long she'd been asleep when a thumping sound awakened her suddenly. Her eyes sprang open, and her heart pounded so hard she wondered whether the sound of her heart beating had woken her.

She heard it again: *thump, thump, thump.* Like heavy footsteps in the hall. She fumbled for the tiny purse-size flashlight she'd placed on the bedside table. When she'd found it and turned it on, she moved the slender beam of light around the room. The thumping sound had come from the hall, however, not her room. She moved the light to the doorway, and just as she did, she thought she saw the doorknob turn. She sat, frozen in her bed, with the light trained on the doorknob. This time, she was certain it had turned.

Her heart beat a wild rhythm in her chest and then seemed to do flip-flops when she saw the door open slightly and heard the shriek of the hinges. There was a pause, and the hinges cried out again as the door opened a little wider.

"Who's there!" Fear made her hoarse.

There was another pause, and then a face appeared around the edge of the door. For a moment, the tiny beam of light made the face appear dead white, but in the next instant, Jane recognized the intruder.

"Hillary! What are you doing?"

"Oh, Jane, thank God you're awake," Hillary said, stepping quickly into the room. She stood there, looking like a character from a Dickens novel in her borrowed nightdress with its high, ruffled neck and long sleeves. "I was trying to be careful about opening the door so I wouldn't wake you."

"Well, you scared the shit out of me!"

"I heard a noise."

"I know, so did I."

Something screamed outside Jane's window. Hillary

made a flying leap and was instantly in the bed next to Jane with the covers pulled over her head. Jane's first instinct was to do the same thing, but curiosity was stronger than her fear. She slipped out of bed and went to the window. Another shriek. She shined the light through the murky glass, but it only reflected back at her. She pressed her face to the window and saw something in the branches of the tree outside her window.

"It's OK, Hillary," she said with a little chuckle. "It's just an owl in the tree."

Hillary peeked out from under the covers, her eyes still wide with fear. "An owl? You're sure?"

"I'm sure."

"I don't care, I'm not going back to my room." She pulled the covers up to her chin.

"For heaven's sake, Hillary!"

"I left my purse in there, though. And with—you know—things roaming around like they do, I'm not sure that's a good idea.

"Things? Ghosts, you mean? You're afraid a ghost is going to steal your purse?"

"We should go back in there and get it."

"We?"

"I'm not going back in there by myself."

"Good night, Hillary." Jane got in bed, turned her back to Hillary, and pulled the blanket over her.

"Jane!"

She tried to ignore her.

"Jane! I've got several credit cards and over a hundred dollars in cash in that purse."

"Ghosts don't need credit cards or cash." Jane's voice was muffled by the covers.

"Jane Ferguson, there are six living people and at least one dead one in this house. One of them might take my purse!"

Jane sat up, feeling weary, resigned. "All right. We'll go get your purse. Then can we please get some sleep?"

Hillary was already out of bed, headed for the door. "Bring your flashlight," she said over her shoulder. She waited until Jane was beside her, then stepped aside for Jane to open the door.

Hillary's edginess was catching, Jane thought, as she opened the door with caution. She stuck her head out first. The hallway was a shadowy weak soup of darkness, made that way by the little bit of light coming from one of the sconces at the end of the hall. She took a step out and stopped. Her sharp intake of breath made a soft, high-pitched sound. A woman dressed in white stood in front of the door to Hillary's room. She fled toward the dark end of the hall, her long white gown flowing behind her. There was no sound of footsteps as she ran, and then she disappeared in the darkness.

"Oh my Lord!" Hillary clutched Jane's arm. "Did you see that? A ghost! Did she have my purse?"

"It can't be a ghost." Jane was hurrying toward the end of the hall where the woman had disappeared.

"Where are you going?" Hillary was still standing in front of the door to Jane's room. She sounded frightened.

"To see if I can find her."

"Jane! It might be dangerous!" Jane ignored her, and in the next second, Hillary was at her side. "You're not leaving me here all alone."

By now they had reached the end of the hall. Jane shined the pinpoint light of her little flashlight first to the right, where the stream of light played across a dingy wall, and then to the left, where it fell upon a doorway. Jane reached for the latch and opened it to what seemed a dark abyss.

"It's the back staircase," Jane said. "Just like the servants used in all those old novels."

"It's dark down there."

Jane shined the light on the rough wooden steps. "She must have gone down there." She started down the steps. "Come on, let's see if we can find her."

"Jane . . ."

"Go back to my room and wait for me if you want to. Or go to your room. I don't think she had your purse." She glanced to her right. Hillary was beside her on the narrow step.

"Wherever that flashlight goes, I'm going."

"All right, but be quiet. We don't want anyone to hear us."

They crept, side by side, down the narrow staircase to a door at the bottom, which opened into a small, closetlike hallway between the kitchen and dining room. Jane shined the light into the cavernous dining room first. It was quiet and deserted except for the chair backs standing at attention along the long table. She aimed the light into the kitchen. It was, by contrast, in disarray, with dishes from the dinner they'd been served earlier stacked on the counter next to an old-fashioned pump. Dirty pots and pans were piled on the servants' table in the middle of the room.

Jane took a step into the kitchen and felt its warm moistness envelop her. In the same instant, a dark form sprang up to rest on top of the table and hissed. Jane quickly took a step backward. She was barely able to suppress a scream, and Hillary was even less successful. They both saw at once, though, that it was Hieronymus protecting her turf.

"Nice kitty." Jane's entreaty was met with a whining growl and a flick of a claw-bared paw. In the same instant, she saw a wisp of white in the shadows and quickly moved the beam of her light toward it just in time to see something or someone disappear through the opened back door into the night.

"She went outdoors," Jane said, hurrying toward the opening.

Hillary once again stuck close to her. "Jane we can't" —water in the rain-soaked grass squished between Jane's toes before Hillary could finish her sentence—"go out there in our bare feet." The rain had stopped, although the air still felt heavy with moisture.

Jane hesitated for a moment and then once again ignored Hillary when she saw the white-clad figure running through the darkness toward a tangled garden.

Jane slogged through the wet grass as fast as she could.

"Jane, don't—"

"This is crazy. I just want to find out what's going on," Jane called over her shoulder. She caught a glimpse of Hillary holding up her nightgown, splashing through the soaked lawn.

"Where's she going?" Hillary called to her.

"Look! She just went in that little house there."

They reached the house, both with muddy, wet feet, and when they were inside, Jane swept the small beam of the flashlight around. An assortment of rakes, hoes, shovels, trowels, and other garden tools hung on the walls and rested on crude wooden tables along with buckets and clay flowerpots.

"Looks like a garden shed," Hillary said. "And looks like the ghost has disappeared again."

Jane continued to shine her light around the room. "She's got to be in here somewhere," she said, in spite of the fact that no one, other than the two of them, was visible. Suddenly she felt something flying past her head and in almost the same second heard a thud. She turned quickly to see the yellow handles of a pair of large gardening shears still quivering from having been thrust into the wall. They had been thrown from somewhere in the darkness, and they had been meant for her head.

5

Jane and Hillary slogged through the soggy garden to the kitchen and up the back stairs. They sat in the darkness on the edge of the bed in Jane's room.

"Those were expensive garden shears, but they've never been used, judging by the look of the garden." Hillary sounded scolding. "It makes you wonder where some people's heads are, doesn't it? Don't they ever watch my show? I mean, I must have devoted at least half a dozen shows to pruning. Remember, Jane? You produced the last one. On pruning to avoid black spot and fungus?"

"Why are we talking about fungus, Hillary? Someone just tried to kill us."

"Not someone, Jane. Some*thing.*"

"Whatever."

"And that's just the whole point. Like I said, people who are careless with their gardening can't be trusted. You just never know what they have in their background. That's why we've got to get out of here, Jane, dear. I am not used to this kind of thing, you know."

"Well, if it makes you feel any better, neither am I. I mean, it's been years since anyone, excuse me, any*thing* tried to impale me with pruning shears."

"That kind of sarcasm doesn't become you, Jane. Don't you realize the seriousness of our situation?"

"Excuse me, are you referring to the unkempt garden or the attempt on our lives?"

"That does it, Jane. There is no place for that kind of attitude at Élégance du Sud. I have tried to be patient with you, even though you are an abominable cook and a disastrous gardener and you have a tin eye when it comes to decorating. But I can only forgive so much. You know that all of my television shows, be they on gardening or decorating or entertaining, are of a positive, upbeat nature, and you know that my interior designs reflect the sheer joy of living, as do my culinary creations. If your attitude doesn't fit, then you will have to seek employment elsewhere."

"Good Lord, Hillary. You waste all that breath. Why don't you just say 'You're fired' and be done with it."

"Very well then, you're fired."

"Fine. Let's get some sleep."

"Fine." Hillary got up, went to her purse and pulled out a sleeping mask, then turned back the already mussed covers and crawled into bed. She slipped the mask over her eyes before she lay down.

"This is my bed, Hillary. Yours is next door. And since I'm no longer employed by—"

"You surely don't expect me to go back to my room, do you?" Hillary said, with her back still turned.

Jane thought of telling Hillary that was exactly what she expected, under the circumstances, but instead, she shrugged. "Silly me." She slid into bed and once again pulled the blanket up to her chin and turned her back to Hillary.

There was a long moment of silence. Finally, Jane spoke. "What the hell is a tin eye, Hillary?"

The only answer was a soft snore. In a little while, Jane, in spite of her anxiety about an attempt on her life, found herself drifting into sleep. Several minutes passed. Then suddenly . . .

"Chester Collins!"

The sound of the name being spoken made Jane bolt

upright to a seated position in bed. She looked around the darkened room, feeling disoriented. "Where?" she said aloud.

"The Reverend Chester Collins!" It was Hillary who had spoken. She, too, was sitting upright.

"You're having a nightmare, Hillary. Go back to sleep."

"No, I'm not having a nightmare."

"If you're dreaming about Chester Collins, it's a nightmare." Chester was the pastor of the Church of God's Riches back home in Prosper and a city alderman as well. His primary interests, Jane had observed, were lining his own pockets and sleeping with his sexy secretary. It didn't make sense that Hillary was talking about him now, but then Hillary often didn't make sense.

"Listen to me, Jane. He may be the only person who can help us."

"You've lost it, Hillary. You've finally completely lost it." Jane lay down in the bed again and pulled the covers over her head.

"He might be able to give us some insight into all the dreadful things that are going on around here. Like something trying to kill us, I mean."

"Chester Collins couldn't give us insight into a paper sack." Jane's voice sounded muffled, even to her own ears, coming from under the covers.

"He's from this part of Alabama, Jane. He's related to the Beans. He knows their history. Maybe he knows why they want to kill us."

Jane flipped the covers off her head. "How do you know so much about Chester Collins? You and I only met him a few months back."

"Yes, yes, I know. I'd never seen him before in my life until you insisted that we interview him because you thought he murdered that poor, unfortunate woman we found quite by accident."

Jane sat up. "Hillary, I never insisted that *we* do anything. And I never said he murdered anyone. I only . . . Oh, never mind. Just tell me. How did you get to know so much about him?"

"Billy told me."

"Billy? Your husband?"

"Yes. It turns out they're both members of the Elks Lodge. But listen, Jane. All we have to do is get in touch with him, and he can help us get out of this mess. I just know he can!"

"How are we going to get in touch with him with the phone lines dead and you without your mobile?"

There was another long silence and then the sound of Hillary sniffling.

"Hillary? Are you crying?"

Another sniffle.

"Ah, come on, Hillary, don't do that." Jane lit the lamp on the table next to the bed. Hillary was still sitting up in bed, wiping her eyes with the edge of the sheet while her sleeping mask rested on her forehead.

"We're going to die here, aren't we? Some inhuman thing is going to kill us."

"Hillary . . ."

"It's just so . . . so *inconvenient*. We're just coming into the wedding season. All those lovely weddings and engagement parties to cater . . ." She had begun to sob.

"Geez, Hillary, maybe I could talk the ghost into waiting until after the wedding season to kill us."

"Could you, Jane? That would be so helpful." She stopped crying and turned toward Jane with a look of gratitude.

"Hillary . . ."

"What?"

"How can I make you understand, we've really got more to worry about than the wedding season and . . . and fungus and black rot?"

"Make *me* understand? You're the one who's making light of this mess we're in. That's why you are no longer employed by Élégance du Sud."

Jane breathed a heavy sigh. "Maybe we ought to just try to go back to sleep. Maybe things will look better in the morning."

"No they won't, and I can't sleep. I just know it."

"Just try, Hillary. We can't do anything about this until morning, and we'll be able to think better if we're rested."

Hillary hesitated, then said reluctantly, "All right. I'll try."

Jane blew out the light and was doing her best to go to sleep again herself. However, it was becoming more difficult to push away the thoughts of someone—or some *thing*—trying to kill them. That they were trapped in such a creepy place didn't help. She felt restless, but she didn't turn over for fear she'd wake Hillary. She lay in silence for several minutes before she realized Hillary wasn't asleep, either.

"Jane . . ."

"Hmmm?"

"I can't sleep."

"Try."

"I am trying."

"Try harder."

"A nice cup of warm milk might do it."

Silence.

"And some of that rhubarb pie we had for dessert. I know there were leftovers."

More silence.

"The cook should have added tart apples. Granny Smiths, maybe. And it could have been served with a brandy sauce."

"Hillary . . ."

"What?"

"Go to sleep."

"Sugary foods actually aid sleep." Another pause. "If you don't want to go to the trouble of making a pie crust, you can make a brown betty with the rhubarb and apples. I like to use that soft French bread with the crust removed."

"Christ, Hillary, just go downstairs and get your warm milk and leftover pie, then let's get some sleep."

"I can't go down there by myself. You have to go with me."

"No I don't. You just fired me, remember?"

"What's that got to do with it? Neither of us should be

alone. Not with dead people walking around flinging things at us. Think of your own safety, Jane, think of—''

Jane sighed heavily. "All right," she said, interrupting Hillary. She flung the covers off once more and sat up, then reached for the flashlight. "I can see I'm not going to get any sleep until we get this over with." She had already started for the door, but she stopped, looking over her shoulder. "Come on."

Hillary pulled her sleeping mask off and scrambled out of bed. "You won't regret this, Jane."

"I already do."

Hillary didn't seem to hear her. "You'll see that I'm right. We have to stick together. And besides, once you've had the hot milk and a little bit of sweets, you'll sleep much better."

With Jane leading the way and holding the lamp, they walked down the hall to the doorway that led to the back staircase. The stairwell seemed even darker this time than it had earlier when they'd seen the ghostly figure there. They both stood at the top of the landing, looking down.

"I can't go down there," Hillary whispered.

"Good." Jane turned away from the stairs. "We'll go back to bed."

"Jane, I *must* have that hot milk."

Jane turned back to Hillary. "Sorry, Hill, but you have to go downstairs to get milk."

"No, I mean I can't go down that staircase. We'll have to go the long way around. Through the front hall."

Jane sighed, reached behind her to close the door, and led the way toward the front staircase. She didn't want to admit it to Hillary, but she was just as glad not to be going down the back stairs herself. She couldn't keep the thought out of her head that the "ghost" they saw could still be lurking in that dark passage.

They made their way as silently as possible down the front stairs, through the hall and dining room, and into the kitchen. The floor was cold to Jane's bare feet, a frozen pond of stone, in spite of the warm, humid air in the house. She set the lamp on the table, and Hillary immediately began opening cupboard doors in the messy kitchen, looking for a clean pan, glasses, and a knife to cut the pie while she kept up her usual litany.

''Copper pots. That's what this place needs. They look wonderful in old-fashioned kitchens with stone floors. But a few modern touches wouldn't hurt, either. Look at that fridge. Hopelessly out of date. And no dishwasher! At least there's a gas stove.'' She was still rummaging around in cupboards. ''Aha! Here's a clean pot. Take it, Jane, and see if there's milk.''

Jane opened the refrigerator. ''Yes, it's here.'' She sniffed it. ''Still smells OK. I don't think the electricity has been off long enough for it to spoil.''

''I think that's a gas-powered refrigerator, Jane. Some people in these remote areas have them because the electricity goes out so often.'' She set the glasses on the cupboard. ''Heat it for me, lamb. I'm going to have to wash some glasses. Now, where's that pie?''

''Do you really think we should be raiding someone else's kitchen?''

''Ah, look! Brandy! I could stir up a quick sauce.''

''Hillary, don't you dare.''

Hillary ignored her. She already had the sugar and butter in a pan and was looking for cream. She was very efficient and soon was stirring it on the stove. She wrinkled her nose. ''Something smells funny.'' She glanced at the pot Jane was overseeing. ''The milk! Jane, you've scorched the milk!''

Jane quickly snatched the pot from the burner, but it was too late. The milk had already turned slightly brown, and she could see, when she tipped the pan, the thick, black coating at the bottom.

Hillary shook her head sadly. ''Jane, Jane, Jane. You can't even heat milk.''

''Of course I can. It's hot, isn't it?''

Hillary took the pot from her, emptied it, and placed it in the sink. ''You'll have to wash this so we can use it again, since there are no more clean ones. There appears to be no hot water downstairs. Just this old-fashioned pump for cold water, so you'll have to heat it in the kettle."

Jane pumped the water into the kettle and set it on the stove. Hillary went back to stirring the brandy sauce.

"Have you thought of a way to get in touch with Reverend Collins?" Hillary asked.

"My best idea is getting Lotus to send him a message with mental telepathy."

Hillary tapped the spoon on the side of the pan with vigor. "I don't know why I bother to ask. You can't take anything seriously."

"Do you have any better ideas?"

"Well . . ."

"We are at the mercy of the storm and BellSouth, Hillary. I see no other choice but to wait for the storm to end and the phones to be repaired. That is, unless the bridge is miraculously restored overnight. And anyway, if I found a way to communicate with anyone outside of this nut house, it wouldn't be Chester Collins."

"We could call Billy, of course, but he's out of town on business, and besides, what good would that do, with the bridge out?"

"My point exactly."

"Besides, he's not related to the Beans."

"Hillary, can you please tell me why being related to the Beans is an asset in this case?"

"I just told you, Chester Collins will know how they think. He might help us get a handle on this family's crazy ways."

"*We* know how they think, Hillary. Like a bunch of nuts."

"There's more to this place than a bunch of nuts." Hillary was cutting the pie and ladling brandy sauce over each piece. There are supposedly dead people walking around. That's not just nutty. That's scary and weird."

"Which sounds like a description of Chester Collins. Only he's scary and weird in a different way. Weird because he's such a caricature of a money-hungry, womanizing preacher. And scary because he takes himself so seriously."

"Still, I think we should try to get in touch with him."

"No."

"Then who?"

"If it were possible to contact someone, which it's not, I'd choose Beau Jackson."

"Beau Jackson? That policeman back in Prosper who has a crush on you?"

"Who says he has a crush on me?"

"He asked you out, didn't he? Twice."

"How do you know that?" Jane felt a momentary shock that her private life was such common knowledge.

"Is that water hot yet?"

"Hillary . . ." A cautionary tone.

Hillary went to the kettle, opened the lid. "Jane! You didn't light the fire under the kettle. Do you see what I mean? You can't even boil water."

"Don't try to change the subject. How do you know—"

"Billy does volunteer work down at the Policemen's Athletic League. That's all I know. Here, pour some more milk. We'll drink it cold."

"So Billy teaches kids how to play basketball. How does that make him privy to who asks me out?"

"My dear, Billy is the one who encouraged Beau to ask you out."

"Oh God, you're telling me he had to be talked into it?"

"Well, Jane, honey, you *are* a Yankee. And anyway, my point is, Beau Jackson is far too sensible to believe in ghosts. He would think we're crazy."

"That makes two of us. And I'm not a Yankee. I'm from California." She was trying not to think of Beau Jackson being coerced into asking her out.

Hillary placed a serving of pie laced with brandy sauce in front of Jane and sat down opposite her. "We're not crazy, Jane." She emphasized her point with her fork. "We saw what we saw."

"But there has to be a logical explanation."

"There's nothing logical about a dead person getting up out of her casket and walking around," Hillary said, sampling the pie.

"She's not dead."

The look Hillary gave her seemed to be one of uncertainty and fear. "She sure looked dead."

"Yes. I'll have to admit, she sure looked dead." Jane tasted the pie, then put down her fork, feeling unsettled. "Maybe none of this is real. Maybe we've gone nuts, too."

"Nuts? I'm afraid they don't 'gree with my schtomach, but a schnifter of that brandy would do nicely."

Jane was startled to see Uncle Bruce entering the kitchen, walking a little unsteadily. He had the look of an aging child playing dress-up in his burgundy bathrobe that once must have been elegant but now was faded and frayed at the sleeves and lapels. It hung like a carelessly thrown drape on his thin frame.

"Oh, hello, Bruce! Please come in and have some pie. I've just made a lovely brandy sauce to go over it." Hillary had immediately turned into the perfect hostess, in spite of the fact that she was in someone else's kitchen.

"Pie? Oh, no thanks. But a snifter of that brandy . . ."

"Oh, of course, of course." Hillary was up, buzzing about the kitchen. "Now, where would I find a snifter?"

"In that cupboard there. Just to the left of the sink. Might as well get three of 'em. Hate to drink alone, you know." Bruce had retrieved the bottle from where Hillary had left it near the stove and was cradling it in his arm like a precious pet. Jane had the feeling he'd had several drinks already, judging from his unsteady gait and the way he slurred his words.

"Three glasses? Well, if you insist." Hillary pulled the glasses from the cupboard. "It might help us relax, since it looks as if we're not going to have the hot milk."

"Ah yes, tha's what I always say. Relaxing. Jus' a bit more there, if you don't mind, madam. That's it. Jus' a little more. Little more."

Hillary handed Bruce a half-full snifter, then poured a splash in two more glasses and handed one to Jane. "I declare, Bruce, a person does need something to help him relax, doesn't he? There is just so much going on around here!" She was rummaging in the cupboards again.

"Going on? What do you mean?" Bruce sniffed the brandy, then took a swallow. He smiled appreciatively.

"Well, there's Cassandra," Jane said, deciding to follow up on Hillary's lead. "I mean, you all must be busy planning her funeral, and with this storm cutting you off from civilization, I'm sure it must be frustrating."

Bruce gave a dismissive wave of his hand as he sipped the brandy again. "Lotus will take care of all that. Getting the phone back, I mean." He swirled the brandy in his glass, staring at it, then took a big gulp. "Ah, Cassandra. I think all that nasty business was completely unnecessary." He reached for the brandy bottle and poured more into his glass.

Jane pushed her glass aside and leaned toward Bruce. "Nasty business?"

Bruce took yet another sip and leaned toward her. "They think I don't know." He spoke in a loud whisper and his breath smelled as if it would be flammable.

"Here you are!" Hillary set a plate of the rhubarb pie covered with brandy sauce in front of Bruce. "You really should try this. You'll be surprised what the brandy sauce does for it. And I was just telling Jane about the Granny Smiths. You can add them to—"

"Bruce, you were saying . . ." Jane sounded annoyed.

"Granny Smith? Do I know her?" Bruce smiled a crooked smile, took another sip, and seemed to be having trouble sitting up straight.

"They're tart apples. Lovely for pies and . . ."

"What is it they think you don't know?"

"Granny Shmiff." Bruce hiccuped loudly. "That's who I don't know. Never had the pleeser, uh, plesher of meeting the lady."

"Bruce! You're such a card! Never had the pleasure!" Hillary laughed her Southern belle throaty laugh and got up to rummage in the cupboards again. "Now, there must be a coffeepot around here somewhere."

"Coffee!" Bruce pointed a finger into the air, then dropped his hand with a thud. "Keeps me awake."

Jane tried again. "Bruce, what about Cassandra? They

think you don't know about Cassandra, remember?''

"They do?'' Bruce looked puzzled. He took the last swallow of his brandy, then looked at the empty glass with an expression of sadness.

"Bruce, you haven't touched your pie, and really the brandy sauce is—''

"Hillary!''

"Yes, Jane?''

Jane stopped short of telling Hillary what she really wanted to say. Instead, she shoved her own plate toward her. "More pie, please,'' she said, hoping to distract her.

"Really, Jane! You haven't eaten your first piece. Don't they teach you Yankees any manners?'' She got up to get the pie.

Jane felt a moment of gratitude that her trick had worked. She turned back to Bruce. "Now, Bruce, tell me what it is they think you don't know about Cassandra.''

Bruce's head hit the table with a thud, his face landing in the pie.

"Bruce?''

There was no answer.

"Oh, dear.'' Hillary turned around from her search for the coffeepot and gave him a look of concern. "What are we going to do?''

Jane breathed a resigned sigh. "We'll have to get him up to bed.'' She already had her arms around his thin frame, pulling him up, but his body collapsed like a banana peel. "Give me a hand,'' she said over her shoulder.

"We can't take him up to his bedroom, Jane. That just isn't proper.''

"What century are you living in, Hillary?''

"What will his wife think?''

"She'll think he's drunk.''

"Really, Jane, I don't understand you at all. You are far, far too direct. It just isn't seemly.'' In spite of her protests, Hillary had flung one of Bruce's arms over her shoulders. "Perhaps if we took her some of the pie with the brandy sauce . . .''

They had managed to get Bruce into the darkened hallway. "Will you forget the pie and brandy sauce, Hillary?"

"Well, I was just—"

They both stopped suddenly when they saw something dark and shadowy moving toward them. Bruce's deflated body drooped between them.

"Oh my goodness!" Hillary whispered. "It's her again. Cassandra! And she's coming toward us."

"I'll take care of Bruce." A voice creaked and a hand reached toward him.

"Lizzie?" Jane felt a moment of relief. "I'm afraid Bruce got himself looped. We were just—"

"I said I'll take care of him." Lizzie all but snatched him from their grasps and put one of his arms around her thin shoulders. It was a practiced gesture, as if she'd done it many times before. "What were you doing down here?"

Hillary spoke before Jane had a chance to get her wits about her. "I was just making a lovely brandy sauce. Although it was a challenge because the kitchen is a bit unorganized. I could help you, you know. We could start by alphabetizing your spices and moving all your baking ingredients to one area. Then, when you're cooking, if you wash as you go, you'll find cleanup so much easier after a meal. I've done several shows on that theme. I don't suppose you've caught one of them, have you?"

Lizzie gave her an icy look, and her eyes were still cold when she turned to Jane. "The two of you would do well to stay away from Bruce. We know how to take care of our own."

"We were only trying to help," Jane replied, but Lizzie was already moving toward the back stairs.

Hillary leaned forward and called to her. "I could show you tomorrow how to organize that kitchen!"

6

Jane awoke the next morning when she hit the floor with a solid thud. Hillary, still asleep and wound into a cocoon of bed covers, had inched her way across the bed, pushing Jane over the edge.

Jane sat up on the floor, startled. "Hillary?"

Hillary's only response was a muffled, "Mmmmpf," as she wound herself tighter in the blanket and sheet she'd pulled away from Jane.

"Hillary, wake up."

Hillary rolled over, flipped her sleeping mask off of one eye. "Not now, Jane, I got almost no sleep last night."

"You got no sleep. Try sleeping on the edge of the bed with no covers."

Hillary lay still for a moment, then pulled the sleeping mask up to her forehead. She gave Jane a curious look. "What are you doing sitting on the floor in my bedroom?"

"This is not your bedroom, and I'm sitting on the floor because you . . . Oh, never mind. Jane picked herself up and, rubbing a sore hip, limped to the window to pull back the curtains. The sky outside was a gray soup clotted with sour-looking darker clouds still oozing rain. More gloom, she thought. She was definitely not in Southern California anymore.

She turned back to Hillary. "I wonder if we're ever going to get out of this place." She sounded depressed, even to her own ears.

Hillary was now sitting up, looking disoriented. Dozens of auburn colored Medussa's snakes stood out from her head. "Is there any coffee? Billy always brings me coffee before I get out of bed in the morning."

Jane picked up Hillary's silk slacks and blouse, which had dried but were in need of pressing. She flung them at her. "Get dressed, Hill. I'm afraid we'll have to go down for our own coffee."

"But I need a shower, and—"

"All right, go ahead, but I'm going to save my shower for later. First, I'm going down to find out if the telephones have been repaired, and if they have been, I'm going to try to find a way out of here."

Hillary now seemed to have accomplished her resurrection completely and was trying to untangle herself from the shrouds. "I'm going with you! I don't want you leaving me up here alone with Cassandra next door. Or *not* next door, whichever the case may be."

Jane had pulled on her tights and was now slipping her tunic top over her head. "I wish we could have gotten more out of Bruce last night before he got so smashed. He knows something about Cassandra. I think I'll have a little talk with him this morning. Maybe he could explain why she's hopping in and out of that casket."

"I don't want to know. I just want to get out of here." Hillary was trying to smooth her hair without the aid of a hairbrush. "It all seems like a bad dream."

"Or a bad movie," Jane added. "I wouldn't be surprised if we next find a crazy woman in the attic—they're everywhere else in the house."

Hillary leaned closer to the mirror. "I simply can't go downstairs looking like this. I've got to have my hairbrush and some makeup. You wait here, and I'll get it from my room." Hillary went to the door, opened it, and peered into the hall as if she expected Cassandra to be there waiting for her. She stepped cautiously out the door but turned back to speak to Jane. "Do you suppose she's in there?" She used her head to indicate Cassandra's room.

"Who knows?" Jane was digging in her purse, trying to find the toothbrush she usually carried with her.

Hillary took a deep breath and said, "OK," as if she was summoning courage, then closed the door. Jane heard her footsteps moving up the hall toward her room. She gave up looking for her toothbrush, put all the items she'd dumped from her purse back inside, and gave her hair a couple of swipes with the hairbrush. She would stop by the bathroom and at least rinse her mouth before going downstairs. She'd probably have time for that before Hillary came back, she thought.

As she stepped out into the hall, she noticed the door to Cassandra's room closed, as well as the door to Hillary's room. In the bathroom, she was surprised to find two sets of towels and two new toothbrushes, still in the cardboard and cellophane packages, all sitting on top of an old-fashioned chest of drawers. An odd act of hospitality on the part of the Bean family, coming on the heels of one of them trying to kill the two of them, Jane thought.

When she had finished in the bathroom, she started back to her room, but curiosity overcame her. She couldn't resist a peek into Cassandra's room. She stopped in front of the door and looked around to make sure no one was watching, then grasped the doorknob. When she tried to push it open, she found it was locked tight. She tried again, pushing harder, but nothing happened. It hadn't been locked before, she knew.

She moved on to Hillary's door. "Hillary?" There was no answer, but the door was ajar, so she pushed it open and peeked inside. "Hillary?"

Still no answer, and she wasn't in her room. Obviously, she had gone back to Jane's room to wait for her and had carelessly left the door open.

Jane closed the door and went to her own room. "You left your door open, Hillary," she said as she opened the door and stepped inside. "I'm surprised you'd do that when you're so afraid of ghosts walking . . ." Jane stopped and looked around. Hillary was not in this room, either. "Hillary?" The silence confirmed what she already knew.

Puzzled, Jane stepped back into the hall and looked in both directions, but Hillary was nowhere in sight. She walked to the end of the hall and opened the door leading to the back stairs, but there was no one in the shadowy stairwell. It wouldn't be like Hillary to step into that dark place alone, anyway. Thinking she must have gone downstairs ahead of her, maybe for the coffee she craved, Jane decided to go down as well, using the front staircase.

At the bottom of the stairs, she stood, looking around, trying to decide what to do. Should she go to the kitchen first to see if Hillary was there, or should she go to the library where there was a telephone and try that? If Hillary was in the kitchen, she was no doubt enjoying her coffee and probably telling Lizzie how to run the place. Lizzie certainly had not appeared to be open to suggestions last night, but that had never stopped Hillary.

Jane turned toward the wide doors leading into the library. What she saw when she pushed the doors open gave her the first surge of hope and encouragement she'd had since she'd set foot in the Beans' house. A telephone repairman was kneeling on the floor, paying homage to the jack on the wall near the floor. Tools hung from his waist like charms against evil technological mishaps. Lotus stood over him, inspecting his work, dressed in another caftan, this one gold lamé. Her orange-red hair was wound into two buns, one over each ear. She looked like an economy-size Princess Leia.

"A telephone repairman! What a welcome sight," Jane said, walking into the room, trying to ignore the eyes of the dead animals. "How wonderful that you would come on a Sunday!"

"We do emergency jobs on weekends," the repairman said without looking at her.

"I trust you slept well," Lotus said.

"Oh, yes." Jane smiled to make the lie seem more credible.

"America Elizabeth's meanderings didn't disturb you?"

"America Elizabeth?"

"Our ghost. Didn't you see her out on the balcony in the storm?"

The telephone repairman dropped something that skittered across the floor. He reached over from his crouched position to retrieve it. Jane still could see nothing except the back of his head and the back of his lizard-skin cowboy boots.

Jane was caught off guard. "On the balcony? In the storm?"

"I don't know how you could have missed her."

"Well, actually I thought it was . . ."

"Thought it was who?" Lotus frowned slightly, as if she was puzzled.

Jane was uncertain how far to take this. "Cassandra?" It came out sounding timid, but it made the telephone repairman drop another tool.

"Cassandra?" Lotus boomed. "Why, she's quite dead."

"So is America Elizabeth, isn't she?"

"Yes, but America Elizabeth had imagination," Lotus said. "Cassandra was dull as a stick."

Jane gave a little shrug. "Well, I don't know. I thought that horoscope column of hers was pretty entertaining."

Lotus's guffaw exhibited all the energy of her two-hundred-plus pounds, then she leaned toward Jane and spoke in a half-whisper as she wagged a finger. "I was the one who wrote those columns for her. She didn't have the foggiest idea how to read an astrology chart."

"Oh, really?"

Lotus shook her head in dismay. "She got herself into that mess. Told the editors of each of those papers she could do it, then came to me for help. And I couldn't let her look like a fool, could I? It would reflect badly on the family, wouldn't it?"

"Oh, I understand completely." Jane did her best to smile again. The last thing she wanted was to say or do anything to displease anyone in this strange family, and the sooner she could get away from them, the better. She turned toward the repairman. "The phone going to be fixed soon?"

"Won't be long." The repairman spoke without raising his head. "Just a broken wire."

"A broken wire? I thought the storm had knocked out the phones along with the electricity," Jane said.

"Nope." The man still spoke without raising his head.

Jane was decidedly puzzled now. "Um, excuse me." She tapped his shoulder. "How did you find out this phone was out? I mean, there was no way anyone could call you to—"

"Computer check," the man said, his head still buried in his work.

"Computer check?"

"Yeah. We can do that at the main building. Check all the phones. This one didn't check out."

"Oh, I see. She found that she was, for some reason, relieved that Lotus hadn't somehow summoned him with her mind. Mundane things like broken wires and computers seemed comforting, under the circumstances. Suddenly, a realization struck her that gave her even more hope than she'd felt before when she realized there'd soon be a telephone connection to the outside world. "You got here this morning, so the bridge must be repaired." She was still speaking to the back of the repairman's head.

"Nope."

"Then how—"

"I live on this side of the bridge, so the company called me for the job." The man stood, stretched his back, with his hands on his hips, and turned around with a smile. "I think I got 'er fixed."

Jane felt a moment of shock when she saw his face. She had seen him somewhere before, but where? Then it came to her. He bore a striking resemblance to the attendant at the roadside gas station where they'd stopped to ask directions.

"Is something wrong, Jane?" Lotus asked.

"No, of course not. I—I was just wondering if you have

a relative who owns a gas station?'' Jane said, turning to the repairman.

"Me? No. I'm not from around here. All my people live in Georgia.'' He hitched up his tool belt and walked away, clanking like a knight in armor.

"We may as well go to breakfast,'' Lotus said, walking toward the door, a moving beam of sunlight in her golden robe.

"I'll be there in a minute,'' Jane said. "I just want to make a quick call.''

"Fine. Breakfast is buffet style until nine o'clock. But Katrin eats all the muffins by eight.'' She slipped her massive frame out the door.

Jane rushed for the telephone. She picked it up and started dialing the Prosper Police Department. She would talk to Beau Jackson about all of this. He could contact the local sheriff about Cassandra's suspicious death, and he could also arrange for some way to rescue them. Before she had finished dialing, she realized that it was Sunday. Beau wouldn't be in the office. He would be at home. She found his home number in the directory, which was on the bottom shelf of the telephone table, and dialed it. The response was the electronic pulsation of a busy signal.

She slammed the receiver down, silently cursing him for being on the phone when she needed him. Frustration was making her edgy. That and the spooky house with its even spookier inhabitants. She took a deep breath to try to regain some composure and reached for the telephone book again. She leafed through it until she found the number for the Taladega County sheriff's office. She dialed the number and waited until a female voice said, "Sheriff's office.'' In the South it sounded like "sherf's office.''

"I want to speak to the sheriff, please.''

Jane heard the same Southern voice, sounding muffled this time, saying, "Lonnie! It's for you, hon.'' A pause, and then, "I don't know who it is. Sounds like a Yankee.''

Several seconds passed before a male voice came on with, "Sheriff Harkelrode here.''

"Sheriff, my name is Jane Ferguson. I'm calling from

the Beans' home, and I want to report that—''

"The Beans? You don't sound like yourself, Katrin. Or is this Lotus?''

"It's neither. My name is Ferguson. Jane Ferguson. I'm a visitor here.''

"Well, I'll swear. Never knew the Beans to have too much company.''

"I'm not company. I'm just . . . Listen, I'm stuck here. My partner and I. We came here to plan a party, and the bridge got washed out, so we can't leave.''

"Party? Has it been a year already? America Elizabeth's having another birthday?''

Jane felt a painful throbbing begin in her temples. "I don't know how long it's been. I just want to know if you can send someone out to repair the bridge so we can leave.''

"Bridge? You mean the one over Sycamore Creek? Just before you turn off on the Beans' road?''

"That's the one.''

"Bridges is not my department. You'll have to call County Maintenance. Hang on, and I'll transfer you.''

"No! Wait! Don't hang up!''

"What? Oh, you still there Miz Ferguson? Say, that name sounds familiar. You wouldn't be any kin to Jim Ed Ferguson that grew up down in Prosper, would you?''

"Yes. I mean, no. But listen, there's something else I need to talk to you about—''

"Too bad. Jim Ed's a good ol' boy.''

"He's that, all right.''

"What?''

"Please, listen to me.'' Jane glanced quickly at the door to make sure no one would overhear. "I want to report . . . well, one of them claimed it was murder, but—''

"You don't mean it. Murder? Not ol' Jim Ed.''

"No, not Jim Ed, it's—''

"Well, thank the Lord. You had me worried there for a minute.''

Jane was feeling desperate, and her head was throbbing

even more. "It's Cassandra. Only I don't think she's really dead."

"Cassie? You're pullin' my leg."

"No, no, I'm very serious."

"Of course Cassie's dead."

"Let me explain—"

"Well, she can't be murdered if she's not dead."

By now, Jane was feeling desperate. "Please, just listen. Lotus said she was murdered, but I've seen her walking around, and then the one they call Uncle Bruce said—"

The sheriff laughed. "Oh, now I get it. Them Beans has been tellin' you stories about their ghosts, I bet."

"Well, yes, but nevertheless, the circumstances are very . . . unusual. And, as I said, Lotus seems to think something is amiss. I think you should come investigate."

"Investigate? Who would I investigate? Cassie died of a heart attack. Seen the coroner's report myself. It's sad when it happens to a young person like that, I grant you, but when there ain't no suspects . . . What do you expect me to do?" The sheriff chuckled.

"I think you should at least talk to Bruce. He hinted that—"

"Don't let them Beans get to you, ma'am. After you been around 'em for awhile, you begin to notice that they're a little bit odd. So my advice to you is just don't pay 'em no mind."

"But—"

"Listen, I'd like to chat with you, but I got police business to take care of. We got an escaped convict on our hands. Guy named Willie Peabody. Got to get the word out all over the county. Anyway, nice talking to you, Miz Ferguson, and I'll check on that bridge repair." There was a click and then the buzz of a dial tone.

Jane felt choked with frustration, and she felt more than a little desperation. She would call Beau Jackson again. He was a savvy policeman who would know what to do, even if Taladega County was out of his jurisdiction. She picked up the telephone to dial his home number again, but there was no dial tone. She tapped the receiver button several times, but nothing happened. It appeared they were once again cut off from the rest of the world.

Maybe there was hope, though. Maybe the telephone repairman was still here. Jane slammed down the receiver and rushed into the hall. No one was in sight, but she heard the sound of voices coming from the dining room.

When she opened the door, she saw only Winston seated at the table. He seemed to be just finishing his plate of food.

"Oh, good morning," Winston said, glancing up from his plate. "I'm afraid you're a little late. All the muffins are gone."

Jane sank down onto one of the chairs. "That's all right. I'm not very hungry, anyway." There was a note of weariness in her voice.

"Where's your friend?" Winston asked, chewing on a piece of bacon.

"Hillary?" Jane looked around as if she were searching for her. "She came down earlier for coffee. She must have gone back to her room."

"Mrs. Scarborough has not been in." It was Lizzie speaking in her crackling voice as she came in, carrying a tray. She picked up dishes from the buffet and placed them on the tray.

"But she must have. She—"

"No, I've been here all morning. She's not been here." Lizzie looked and sounded as if she defied anyone to disagree with her.

"Oh, a late sleeper is she?" Winston chuckled. "Doesn't pay to do that, you know. Not if you want a muffin."

"Mrs. Scarborough is too late for breakfast, but you will send her down anyway to plan the party." Lizzie sounded authoritative and slightly menacing.

"Oh, no," Jane said. "I'm afraid we won't be able to plan the party now. You see, we have to get back to—"

"There will be no getting back. Not with the bridge out. We'll have the party. You will plan it. All those on this side of the bridge will come." With those words, Lizzie walked out of the kitchen carrying the tray loaded with dishes. Jane watched her leave, feeling more than a little intimidated.

She left the dining room without even so much as a cup of coffee and walked up the stairs, depressed and worried about Hillary. If she wasn't in her room and hadn't come down to breakfast, where could she be?

Jane walked up the hall, thinking she would check Hillary's room again when she saw the door to the back stairway open. In a few seconds, Hillary stuck her head into the hall with caution.

"Hillary!" Jane called to her. "What are you doing in that stairwell? I thought you were scared to go down there."

"Jane, you're not going to believe this." Hillary was walking toward her. She looked disheveled and pale, and dirt smudged her arms and face.

"Not going to believe what?"

"I've been in the cellar."

"In the cellar?" Jane was puzzled. "How on earth did you end up there?"

"There's a secret passage."

"Oh God. I can't believe it."

"That's what I *said*. You're not going to believe it. My hairbrush fell behind the bureau in my room, and when I tried to move it to get the brush, it opened up into this passageway."

"And you went into it?"

"I didn't mean to." Hillary was speaking in a desperate whisper, and she was shaking as she spoke. "I just accidentally knocked my brush down onto one of the stairs, and when I stepped in to get it, the bureau closed behind me."

"I don't understand. How did the bureau close?"

Hillary shook her head. "I don't know. There's some sort of moveable contraption on the floor where the bureau sits, I think, but listen to this: There were dust bunnies and cobwebs you wouldn't believe. They can easily be taken care of with a lamb's wool wand. But that's not the worst part.''

''Worse than dust bunnies? What could it possibly be?''

''Bruce. He's down there in the cellar, and he's dead.''

7

Jane paced the floor in Hillary's room while Hillary, still pale and shaking, sat on the bed. "Are you absolutely sure Bruce is dead? Maybe he's just plastered again."

Hillary shook her head. "He's dead. I'm sure."

"How can you be sure?" There was an edge to Jane's voice.

"Well, for heaven's sake, Jane, when I asked him if he would like another chance to sample my brandy sauce, he didn't say a word. No one who's alive and breathing would be able to pass up an offer like that."

Jane rolled her eyes and turned toward the bureau. "Come on, we'd better get the poor boozer out of the cellar before he catches his death."

"Jane, I told you. He's already—"

"Is this how you said you got down there?" Jane was tugging at the bureau.

"Yes, but I'm not going down there again."

With one solid pull, Jane had the bureau out from the wall. The slightly sweet scent of damp, musty earth wafted up from the darkness. "I'd better get my flashlight," she said, letting the bureau settle back to its position against the wall.

Hillary followed her to her room to get the flashlight, then helped her move the bureau again.

OK,'' Jane said. ''You wait here. I'll be right back.'' She took a tentative step into the abyss, keeping a hand on the bureau.

''Don't leave me up here alone,'' Hillary said.

''OK,'' Jane said, turning around to get a better grip on the bureau. ''Put that vanity chair behind the bureau so it won't close all the way.''

Hillary moved the chair, and Jane reached for her hand, secretly glad that she wasn't going to have to walk into that black hole alone.

Jane aimed the small beam of light on the step in front of her. It illuminated no more than a step at a time. ''Geez, it's really spooky in here. I can hardly see what I'm doing with this little flashlight. How'd you ever make it down these stairs with the doorway closed?''

''I didn't have any other choice, did I?'' Hillary's voice trembled, and she gripped Jane's hand so hard, Jane's own hand began to feel numb. ''I mean the doorway was closed, and I just had to keep going, even though I couldn't see a thing. Oh, my Lord! Just look at the cobwebs I walked through.''

They made their way around two landings and were almost at the bottom of the stairs. Jane could barely make out shadowy forms of shelves filled with an odd assortment of household items on them, including an old toaster, a lantern, a box of matches, several jars of canned goods, a broken clock. ''Where's Bruce? I don't see him anywhere.''

''He's over by the cellar doors.'' Hillary was whispering, and she was pulling back on Jane's hand, reluctant to go any farther.

''How on earth did you ever see him in this darkness?''

''There's more light over yonder by the door. There's light streaming down through the cracks in the wood. That's where he is.''

Jane stepped off the bottom step onto the hard-packed, earthen floor. ''You mean he's just lying on the—'' What she saw made her suck in her breath and lose her voice. Someone—it looked like Bruce—was lying on the floor. She stared at him for a long moment. "Bruce?" Her voice had returned, but she found she couldn't speak louder than a hoarse whisper. She was aware of Hillary cringing behind her. Jane took another step closer. "Bruce?" she said again. There was no response. He lay there, still as death itself. Jane leaned over him, and a little scream escaped her throat when she saw his dead eyes.

Her scream startled Hillary, who screamed as well and threw her arms around Jane, holding on as if she were drowning in her own fear. Jane held on to Hillary and screamed again, too. Finally they pulled apart and looked at each other, wide-eyed and frightened.

Hillary spoke first, an urgent sound. "I was right, wasn't I? He's dead, isn't he?"

Jane nodded. "He's dead," she managed to say. Nevertheless, she leaned over and felt for a pulse at his throat. "He's dead," she said again. She noticed a sour smell, as if he'd thrown up, and there was, in fact, a bit of it still on his shirt front.

"Maybe he fell down the stairs."

Jane shook her head. "Not likely. He's a long way from the foot of the stairs. And look." She used the light beam to point. "There's something on the front of his shirt. I think he threw up."

"Disgusting!"

Jane turned back to Hillary. "Someone dragged him down here."

Hillary shuddered. "Oh my Lord, Jane. How could you possibly know something like that? You know how drunk he was. He probably just stumbled."

Jane shook her head. "Look at his shoes. See the scuff marks on the toes? I think someone dragged him down the stairs." She turned around, shining her light on the earthen floor. "Look. There's just barely enough light to make out the ridges in the dirt where his shoes must have dragged along."

"But why would anyone put him down here?" There

was a note of desperation in Hillary's voice, as if she was hanging onto the idea that Bruce stumbled to his death.

"Maybe because whoever dragged him killed him, and they wanted to get him out of the way so no one would know." Jane turned to Hillary and grasped her arm. "And they'll be back. Obviously, you can't leave a dead body lying around like this. They'll want to move him before decomposition sets in."

"They? Who's they?" Hillary was beginning to sound frantic.

"A family member, I guess, since there's no one else around. And that means we've got to get out of this cellar before the killer comes back and sees us and we end up like Bruce."

"Oh Lord, Jane, you've done it again. You've gotten us into another mess."

"*I've* gotten us into a mess? It wasn't my idea to come here."

"Well, I never in my life ran into dead bodies before I met you."

"Hillary, I suppose you think I—" A noise from above the cellar door stopped Jane. She grabbed Hillary's hand. "Let's get out of here," she whispered.

Together, they scrambled up the stairs, around both landings, and into the bedroom. When they moved the chair that was blocking the bureau, it slammed shut with a loud thud. Jane and Hillary stared at each other for a moment, too frightened to speak.

Finally, Jane moved toward the door. "We've got to tell someone about this."

"Who?" Hillary seemed to be unable to move.

Jane turned back to her. She felt a moment of panic. Who *could* they tell? Who could they trust?

A little color had come back into Hillary's face. "Maybe the phone is working now," she said. "Maybe we could call the sheriff."

Jane shook her head. "No, it's not working. There was a repairman here earlier. He said there was a broken wire, and he fixed it temporarily, but it's out again."

"A broken wire?" Hillary rushed to the closet and pulled out her handbag. "Let's go downstairs, Jane."

"But . . ."

"Come on," Hillary said, opening the door to the hall. "I'm not going down there alone." She was out the door, and Jane had to rush to keep up with her.

"Hillary, where are you going?"

"Why didn't you tell me it wasn't the storm that knocked out the phone?" Hillary was hurrying down the hall, the heels she wore with her once-pressed silk slacks clacking out a busy staccato. "A broken wire? Is that all? For heaven's sake, Jane."

Jane followed Hillary as she hurried down the front stairs. "I don't know what you're up to, Hillary, but I hope you know as long as we're in this house you have to be careful. These people are—"

Hillary was well ahead of her. At the bottom of the landing, she turned and headed toward the library's wide double doors. Jane caught up with her and was directly behind her when she pushed the doors open. Lotus was standing near the fireplace working on a large painting and speaking in a hushed voice to Hieronymus, her cat, who was perched on the mantel. She put down her brush and picked up the cat and stroked her fur, and as she turned around, the mass of heavy, dark beads cascading down her bosom made a clicking sound, like mice on stone floors. A look of surprise marked her face when she saw the two of them enter.

"Oh, Lotus, the most awful thing has happened!" Hillary rushed toward the big woman, her hands up in the air, making mauve-tipped, upside down exclamation marks. She stopped, looking at Lotus's painting. It was almost a life-size rendition of a somber looking woman with a shawl over her head.

"It's America Elizabeth," Lotus said, following Hillary's stare and glancing at the painting. "I'm having trouble with the eyes." She turned back to Hillary. "What terrible thing?"

Hillary launched into her story before Jane could decide

how much they should reveal to her. "It's poor Bruce. I'm afraid he's passed on to the other side."

"Passed on to...? Lotus seemed puzzled, then her heavy jowls dimpled as a smile lit up her face. "Oh good, they fixed the bridge."

"No, no, the poor man is dead." Hillary managed to give the last word two syllables.

"Dead?" Lotus pronounced the word in exactly the same way. "Oh my Lord! No!"

Hillary nodded. "In the basement. We just found him."

Lotus's eyes filled with tears. "I should have warned him. It's all my fault!"

"Warned him about what?" Jane asked.

Lotus turned away, pacing, still crying. "I—I don't know. I had this funny feeling last night."

"I think we need to notify the sheriff," Jane said, eyeing the cat.

"But the telephone is dead again." Lotus put the cat down and wound her beads around her hand nervously. The cat followed Jane with its eyes and gathered itself to pounce. "That repairman didn't fix it," Lotus continued. "And...and he's...gone. And now you say poor uncle Bruce is..." Her voice quivered with grief.

"The repairman gone?" Jane said. "But he said he lives on this side of the bridge. All we have to do is find him and bring him back to the house."

Lotus put her hands to her temples and closed her eyes, frowning as if she had a headache. "No, no, he's not really gone, but he's..."

"What?" Jane was staring intently at Lotus, trying to discern what she was saying, and she was only vaguely aware that Hillary had moved away from her.

Lotus shook her head and looked as if she was about to cry. "I can't quite see, but..."

"See what?" Jane was still puzzled.

Lotus's hands flew up in a gesture of despair. "I don't know. Sometimes I just don't get the psychic messages right. Like about poor Uncle Bruce. I wasn't sure. I thought I was wrong."

"OK, listen," Jane said in a firm, no-nonsense voice, "we've got to find some way to notify the sheriff, and I don't think psychic messages are an option. Is there any way out of here? Through the woods? A back way? Any way at all that doesn't involve crossing the creek?"

"No." Lotus was crying now, wiping her eyes with the end of her tunic. "We're isolated here. Our ancestors planned it that way. And now, poor Uncle Bruce . . . Oh dear, what are we going to do?"

"That should do it!" Hillary was sitting on the floor on the opposite side of the room. She held a Swiss Army knife in her right hand, waving it as if it were a banner.

"Hillary, what on earth are you doing?" Jane asked.

Hillary stood up, picked up her handbag, and dropped the knife inside. "I just fixed the telephone."

"You fixed the—"

"Some repairman they sent out here. He didn't seem to know the terminal has to be tightened once the wire is attached. That's why it worked for a while and then stopped working."

"How do you know this stuff, Hillary?" Jane was looking at her, amazed.

"Didn't you watch my show on home repairs last spring? It was before I hired you, of course, but you *must* have seen it. Remember, I talked about plumbing, electrical wiring, roof repair, building additions?" Hillary picked up the telephone and put it to her ear. "Dial tone!" Her voice was bell-like as she handed the receiver to Jane.

Jane took the receiver from her, still too amazed to speak. The cat, she noticed with some relief, had lost interest and had curled herself into a snail shape under the sofa. Jane glanced at Lotus, who had collapsed on one of the antique horsehair sofas. Her plump face was crumpled with grief.

"You want to call the sheriff, Lotus? After all, Bruce is your uncle." Jane held the receiver out to her.

Lotus shook her head. "I wouldn't know what to say."

Jane found the number again and dialed the office.

"You again?" the sheriff said when she told him her name. "What's the ghost done this time?" Jane could hear a muffled snickering, as if he was trying to conceal it with a not-too-well-placed hand over the mouthpiece. She could imagine him raising his eyebrows at whoever might be in the office with him, in a conspiracy of merriment.

"We found Bruce dead in the cellar this morning." Jane blurted the message out, partly in anger at him for not taking her seriously and partly because she was too upset to think of any other way to do it.

"What!" She knew by the sound of that one word that she had gotten his attention.

"It's Bruce. He's in the cellar. Dead."

"Oh, Bruce." There was a note of relief in his voice. "He been on the sauce again? Probably just passed out. Give him a little time to sleep it off."

"There's no pulse, sheriff, and his eyes are set."

There was another muffled sound. This time it sounded like swearing. "All right." The sheriff's voice came back clear on the phone. "I got to come out with a coroner. That's the law when a person dies at home. That means a helicopter since that damn bridge is out. Do you know what one helicopter trip does to my budget? Do you know what it costs the taxpayers?"

"Sorry to inconvenience you. Bruce should have checked the county budget first." Jane made no attempt to keep the sarcasm out of her voice.

"I'll be out as soon as I can," the disgruntled sheriff said, then there was another muffled tirade that began with "Goddamned Beans."

Jane hung up the phone. "He's coming out in a helicopter. Maybe we can hitch a ride back with him, Hillary."

Before Hillary could reply, Lotus spoke from where she sat on the couch, trying to sniff back tears. "They do that all the time. Send out helicopters, I mean. Because we're so isolated."

"Where do they land?" Jane asked.

Lotus used her pudgy hand to point to the west window. "In that field over there, just behind the graveyard." She shook her head. "I hate them. The sound disturbs my psychic vibes."

"Since we don't all get psychic vibes, you need to make sure your telephone stays in working order," Hillary said. "You should insist on a more competent repairman. Why, I wouldn't be surprised if this one was even lying about that bridge being out."

"Lying?" Jane said. "Why would he do that?"

"Well!" Hillary huffed. "What do you expect from a repairman who doesn't know how to fix a telephone? Obviously, he hadn't had proper training. There's no doubt he never watched my show."

Jane's impatience got the best of her. "For Christ's sake, Hillary, morality and competence aren't decided according to who watches your show."

Hillary stiffened. "Competence can certainly be enhanced in several areas by tuning in regularly."

"I suppose you're going to hint that he doesn't prune his roses, either."

"Prune his roses?" Lotus seemed genuinely puzzled.

"She's trying to trick me," Hillary said, pointing a finger at Jane. Her usually well-manicured nails were beginning to chip, Jane noticed. "She does that because she's one of those tricky lawyers."

"I'm not a lawyer, Hillary, just a law school dropout. Until I make enough money to go back, at least. And I'm not trying to trick you." Jane sat down on the sofa next to Lotus, a weary gesture. "Forgive me for being flip with you, Hillary. I'm a little edgy."

Hillary gave a dismissive wave with her now less-than-perfect hand. "We're both edgy. It's because we haven't had breakfast." She brightened. "Actually, it's a little late for breakfast now, but I can make a lovely pecan and cranberry quick bread that's perfect for brunch along with a corn custard, which is an absolutely marvelous way to have your eggs, especially when you use just a little bit of the gorgonzola as a streusel. Of course, if you don't have gorgonzola, another cheese will do as long as it's—"

"Brunch?" Lotus's face lit up.

"Who is going to take the sheriff down to the basement?" Jane asked. "I'm sure he'll want to question you,

Hillary, because you found the body, but I think a member of the family should be present. And you've got to tell the others, of course.''

Lotus looked distraught. ''I know, but I can't do it by myself. Aunt Julia will be so upset.''

''Jane is really very good at that kind of thing,'' Hillary said as she pulled a slip of paper and a pen from her handbag.

''Me?'' Jane said.

''About that brunch . . .'' Lotus said.

Hillary raised her eyes from the paper she'd been scribbling on. ''Yes, Jane, you can handle the sheriff, can't you? I'm going to prepare brunch. Then you can break the news to Aunt Julia.''

''Me?'' Jane said again.

''You're very competent at that sort of thing, Jane, dear, and besides, I pay you good money to handle details for me.'' Hillary was still distracted by whatever she was writing.

Jane narrowed her eyes at Hillary. ''You fired me, remember?''

''Sometimes you get absolutely obsessive about bearing a grudge, Jane.'' She scribbled some more on the paper. ''Now, let's see, besides the cheese, I'll need buttermilk and eggs and cornmeal.''

''We have that.'' Lotus sounded eager. ''We have all of that. We have to keep the pantry well stocked, being so isolated.

''Good.'' Hillary advanced toward the door, pen and paper still in hand. ''To make things really festive, we should have champagne with orange juice, but if you don't have champagne, we'll make do. Oh, and a nice black bean salad would be nice.''

''Oh, yes!'' Lotus stood and followed Hillary to the door. ''And lots of butter for the cranberry and pecan bread.''

''Of course,'' Hillary said as she walked out into the hall, headed for the kitchen with Lotus close behind. ''And sliced tomatoes. Even if they're not in season, you can make hothouse tomatoes tasty with a little lemon juice and cilantro, and of course we'll need . . .''

Their voices died away as Jane found herself alone in the library. She'd gotten nowhere in her quest to find out what might have happened to Bruce, and now she was stuck with breaking the news to Julia and dealing with the sheriff. But maybe she wouldn't have to worry about any of this much longer. Maybe she could just leave it in the hands of the sheriff and hitch a ride back to the real world in his helicopter.

She couldn't completely rid herself of the nagging feeling that leaving anything in the hands of Sheriff Harkelrode was not a good idea. She glanced at the phone. She could call Beau Jackson. He would know what to do. She picked up the receiver, then put it down again. This was all going to be over soon. There was no need to call anyone. Still, she had a need to talk to someone who wasn't crazy. Someone who wasn't a Bean. She picked up the phone again and dialed his home number. He would most likely be at home, since he had weekends off, unless there was an emergency, and emergencies in Prosper were rare. The phone rang several times before she got his answering machine telling her to leave a message. Feeling frustrated, she dialed the number for the Prosper Police Department.

Naomi Marshall answered the phone with her husky cigarette voice.

"Beau Jackson, please," Jane said.

"Jane? Is that you, hon?"

Jane was momentarily embarrassed. Had she called Beau's office so much she could now be recognized? But that couldn't be true. She'd called no more than twice. "Yes," she finally managed to say, "this is Jane Ferguson."

"I knew it was you, hon. It's that Yankee accent you got. But listen, Beau's not available. He's in a meeting with some other police officers that come down from Birmingham. It's about that escaped convict."

"Oh, I see . . ."

"I'll have him call you."

"No, no. That's all right. I'll just—"

"We got this new caller ID here at the office, and I see you're not at home. Oh Lordy, you're at the Beans'?"

"Why yes, I am, but—"

"Listen, hon, you be careful. Them Beans is kind of odd."

"I'll be careful, but listen, maybe there is something you can do. The bridge has been washed out here, and—"

"Don't the Beans live way up there in Taladega County?"

"Yes, they do. Listen, I don't know who to call here in this county for road work, but Beau will know, so I'd like you to ask him to call someone who can get a road crew out here as soon as—"

"Lord a mercy. I hope you haven't been kidnapped or something."

"Kidnapped? Why would you say that?"

"Don't you know, hon?"

"Know what?"

"Well, Taladega County is where that escaped con is supposed to be."

"I'm perfectly safe, Naomi. No one can get in or out of here."

"Well, you're lucky if that's true. I'll tell Beau you called, and you get home as soon as you can, you hear? I gotta go now. There's another call coming in."

"Naomi! Wait!"

Jane's plea did no good. The connection was severed.

8

Word about Hillary's brunch got around to all the Beans with an efficiency that surprised Jane. By the time she got to the dining room, most of them were assembled there. As Jane saw it, it was at least an opportunity to have everyone together so Lotus could tell them about Bruce as well as the sheriff's imminent arrival.

"Lovely idea, this brunch." Winston poured himself more orange juice. "Especially since all of the muffins were gone by the time I got down for breakfast." He shot an accusing glance toward Katrin.

Katrin had time to deliver no more than a nasty glance in response before the door leading to the kitchen swung open and Hillary, looking regal in spite of her wrinkled silk slacks, emerged carrying a steaming dish. It had to be the corn pudding. To Jane, it looked like a quiche with a cornbread crust.

Lotus followed behind Hillary, carrying a basket with two loaves of the cranberry bread. Lizzie was behind her with the black bean salad. The culinary parade was met with a chorus of sighs.

Julia, however, had not joined the chorus. She sat at the end of the table twisting her handkerchief. When she spoke, her voice was weak and trembling. "Has anyone seen Bruce?" she said after a while.

Jane shot her a quick glance, and then turned to Lotus, waiting for her to speak. Lotus said nothing, however. Her cheeks, full of corn pudding, were bulging and grinding.

Katrin had given her Aunt Julia a quick, nervous glance when she spoke. She turned back to Winston with her cold glare. "Wasn't he with you early this morning, Winston? I thought I saw the two of you going into the kitchen about five o'clock."

"Five o'clock? Good Lord, why would I be up that early?" He cocked his head and scrutinized Katrin. Some of us do get up early to get a head start on the muffins, it seems." Winston gave her a fake smile.

"And some of us lie in bed until late morning and then wonder why there's nothing left." Neither Katrin's voice nor her mouth even suggested a smile.

Winston laughed, an empty sound. "Ah, my dear Katrin, you are so delightfully illogical. How could I be up at five and lying in bed at the same time?" As he spoke, he slashed ruthlessly at the loaf of cranberry bread, until a ragged slice surrendered into his palm.

"Silly me. Of course you probably don't have the strength to rise until noon, since you are so undernourished, never getting any muffins." As she said the word "muffins," she stabbed the butter aggressively with the end of the butter knife.

"Cousin Katrin, first it was late morning and then it was noon. How you exaggerate, my dear. Unusual in a person so lacking in imagination." There was another imitation smile aimed at Katrin, but his eyes were like cold steel.

Katrin's eyes, equally cold, clashed with Winston's, glittering as she parried. "Perhaps you're right about my lacking imagination, dear cousin. I certainly can't imagine you doing anything but complaining."

"Oh dear!" Julia's voice was full of worry and distress. That plaintive sound made Jane squirm in her seat. Everyone turned to look at Julia. "In the kitchen?" she asked, sounding timid. "You say Bruce was in the kitchen?"

"Lotus . . ." Jane began.

Lotus looked at her from the corner of her eyes. Her mouth was open, ready to receive another generous scoop of corn pudding, which now hung suspended on her fork like cargo ready to be loaded.

Jane cleared her throat and spoke again. "Lotus . . ."

Lotus put the still-loaded fork down, took a sip of water, and whispered, "I can't." There was desperation in those two words.

"Can't what?" Julia said.

Winston glanced at Lotus, and his mouth made a moue. "Can't eat any more? Cousin Lotus, that's not like you. Oh, I'll bet the nasty old storm upset you, didn't it? Here, have a bit more corn pudding. Make you feel better. You too, Jane. Just a wee bit more?"

Jane shook her head and glanced at Julia, who sat looking bewildered and near tears. Lotus then burst into tears herself and got up suddenly, disappearing in a hurried waddle into the kitchen.

"Has something happened to Bruce?" Julia's voice was choked with fear. "Why doesn't someone tell me what's going on?"

Winston and Katrin both stared at her, speechless. Jane squirmed uncomfortably in her chair and then finally managed to speak. "Julia . . ." She swallowed hard and tried again. "Julia, I'm afraid something *has* happened to Bruce."

Julia caught her breath and brought her handkerchief to her mouth while her eyes, filled with dread, locked with Jane's.

"He's . . ." Jane glanced at the kitchen door again, wanting to scream for Lotus or Hillary. "Well, I'm afraid he's . . ."

"Has Uncle Bruce had too much to drink? Has he passed out?" Winston's voice was soft and soothing. "Is that what you're trying to tell Aunt Julia?"

Jane glanced from Winston to Katrin, whose cold blue eyes were now locked onto Jane, waiting.

"Bruce is . . . has passed away." Jane had, in the flash

of a second, decided to use the more euphemistic term rather than say "dead," in the hope that it would soften the blow. Julia, however, had turned as white as the table-cloth, and she looked for a moment as if she might faint.

"Uncle Bruce?" Katrin sounded stunned.

"You found him?" Winston asked.

"Yes, in the cellar."

"In the cellar?" Katrin sounded as if she didn't believe that was possible.

"Are you sure he's dead?" Winston asked. "Sometimes the light shinning through the cracks in the cellar can play tricks. I mean, maybe he just looked that way because he passed out and fell on the floor. Uncle Bruce is a bit of a tippler, you know."

"He's dead," Jane assured him. I've notified the sheriff. He'll be here as soon as he can arrange for a helicopter."

Katrin let out a little cry and jumped up suddenly to go to Julia, who still looked as if she was about to faint. Julia collapsed in her arms. Winston, too, hurried to Julia's side.

"Aunt Julia!" Winston took her into his arms. "Let me help you up to your room. You must lie down. I'll have Aunt Lizzie send you up some tea. Katrin, go to the kitchen and tell Aunt Lizzie we need tea."

He led a weeping Julia out of the room, murmuring words of comfort to her. Katrin, still looking stunned, went into the kitchen. Jane found herself alone at the table, staring at the remnants of Hillary's corn pudding.

She was still sitting there, wondering if she'd done the right thing, when Hillary emerged from the kitchen. Lotus and Lizzie were behind her, and Katrin behind the two of them, carrying a tray with a teapot and cup. Katrin left through the wide doors leading to the stairway to take the tea up to Julia.

Hillary looked at Jane. "Katrin said you told them."

Jane nodded.

Lotus sat down at the table again and picked up a buttered slice of cranberry bread to munch while she wept. Lizzie had begun to clear the table, except for Lotus's plate.

Her expression was frozen, but then it was always cold, Jane thought.

"Did you tell Lizzie?" she asked Hillary.

"Of course," Hillary said.

"I told her," Lotus said at the same time, the words coming out muffled and chewed, along with crumbs from the bread.

Jane gave Hillary an accusing look.

Hillary squirmed a little. "Well . . ." Then she brightened. "At least they know now."

Jane didn't respond. She was wondering if she had, after all, done the right thing. Whoever killed Bruce was in the house and, no doubt, was at the table when she told them about finding the body. Would that put her in danger? Now she wished she'd waited until the sheriff arrived. But would she feel any safer with the sheriff there? He hadn't come across as particularly competent when she'd spoken with him on the phone. In spite of her uneasiness, she still felt it was right to have told Julia the truth as soon as possible.

Jane shook her head, still feeling uncertain as well as sad for what she'd had to do. She got up and started helping Lizzie clear the table.

Hillary picked up a plate. "The sheriff should be here any minute now, and we're just not going to listen to any nonsense about it being against policy to take us back to Prosper in his helicopter," she insisted, scraping the remnants of the plate onto a platter.

"You're going back to Prosper?" Lotus asked, reaching for another spoonful of the corn pudding just before Lizzie picked up the dish.

"Oh yes. As soon as possible." Hillary sounded confident.

"But what about the party?" Lizzie and Lotus said in unison. Lotus stopped her chewing, and Lizzie paused in midstep between the table and the kitchen.

"Party?" Hillary seemed surprised they would mention it. Jane shared her surprise, given the circumstances.

"Why, yes." Lotus swallowed hard. "America Elizabeth's birthday. We couldn't forget that!"

"But you've just had a death—no, *two* deaths in the family!" Hillary was aghast. Her sense of Southern proprieties had obviously been offended. Jane, though surprised as well, said nothing.

"We *never* forget America Elizabeth's birthday." The statement, coming from the usually silent and taciturn Lizzie, was startling.

Lotus dabbed her mouth with her napkin, having chewed and swallowed the last morsel of food that would be allowed her from this table. "That *is* what you came out here for—to plan America Elizabeth's party, you know."

"Well, my goodness, y'all! There will be a decent period of mourning, won't there?" Hillary held up her hands. "I know, I know, Cassandra would want the party to go on. But what about Bruce? What about poor Julia? Can't you see the woman's grieving? You can't have a *party.*"

"Well . . ." Lotus seemed about to relent. Lizzie had let her shoulders droop.

Hillary pressed her advantage, since, obviously, she was as anxious to be done with the Beans and leave as Jane was. "And besides, with the bridge washed out, no one could get here."

"There are several families on this side of the bridge besides us." Lotus's tone was lame, almost pleading.

"A wake," Lizzie said. Everyone glanced at her, but she simply stared back, saying no more.

"Of course!" Lotus said finally, clapping her fat, paint-stained hands together. "A wake! For Uncle Bruce. And for Cassandra, too. We could make it a double." She turned to Hillary. "And you could cater it!"

"Cater a wake?" Hillary shook her head. "I'm afraid that's impossible. I—"

"Well, all right, you don't have to cater it." Lotus stood up, bouncing with enthusiasm. "You could just help us plan it, couldn't you? We can do it tomorrow night."

"We're leaving with the sheriff, remember?" Jane said. "So you'd better plan fast."

Lotus turned to Hillary. "What do we do? Finger sandwiches and punch, or—"

"Oh, my Lord, no!" Hillary was once again aghast. "Finger sandwiches? Why, hon, that's so unoriginal. You should start with cold antipasti, and then a nice hot prosciutto panini—well, if you don't have prosciutto, that lovely ham I saw in the fridge will do, and you can make the focaccia bread. I'll show you how."

Hillary, in spite of her earlier protest, could never, in the end, resist planning a party. Maybe it would at least keep her occupied for the few minutes until the sheriff arrived and they could leave with him.

"Now, if we just had a bit of Fontina cheese," Hillary continued. She put her chipped nail to her pursed lips. "Let's see, what can we substitute? Umm, I'll have another look in the kitchen. Oh!" Her finger went up in the air. "I did notice you have escarole. I have a wonderful recipe using that in a soup with white beans and—"

"Chester Collins!" It was Aunt Lizzie again with one of her rare pronouncements.

"Chester Collins?" Hillary and Jane asked in unison.

"Why, of course, Aunt Lizzie. Of course! That would be perfect!" Lotus seemed ecstatic with enthusiasm. She turned to Jane and Hillary. "We have to have a minister at the wake, you know, and Cousin Chester—he's only a third cousin on Mother's side—is visiting his family just the other side of the woods. He's a minister of the gospel, you see."

"Oh, yes," Jane said, "we know." After the one encounter she'd had with Chester in Prosper, she'd come to think of him as living by the Gospel According to Chester Collins, in which the first commandment was "Thou shalt line thy pockets at every opportunity," and the second was "Thou shalt lie with the women of the land."

Lotus turned back to Lizzie. "Cousin Chester can make the little speech about America Elizabeth, too, can't he?"

"Winston likes to make speeches," Lizzie said, busying herself scraping plates.

Lotus sighed. "Oh yes," she said, nodding at Jane and Hillary, "Cousin Winston always likes to have center stage."

"What little speech about America Elizabeth?" Jane asked.

"About her life," Lotus said. "Oh, I know we'll all be in mourning, but we really must acknowledge her birthday. And there's always that tribute to her read at the party. It's a tradition."

"What about the decor? Should we do everything in black?" Hillary had a pensive frown on her face.

"Decor?" Jane was aghast. "Hillary, this is a wake we're talking about. You don't decorate for a wake."

"Thematic touches are always appropriate for any occasion, Jane." Hillary sat down at the table and began ticking things off on her fingers. "Let's see, I could show you how to make a lovely wreath from the small branches of that grapevine I saw at the side of the house and intertwine it with foxglove that I saw growing in the front. Tasteful and not too festive. Vases of white flowers, of course. I'll have to have a look at what's in your garden, since a florist is out of the question. You should send invitations on parchment, which I could make myself if there were time. But since there's not, we'll see what we have. Oh and bunting."

"Bunting? For a wake?" Jane frowned with astonishment.

Hillary was too absorbed in her planning to notice Jane. "Black crepe paper would be perfect, but I don't suppose you have that."

Lotus shook her head.

"Well, never mind, I know a really clever trick with sheets, and white, of course, is perfectly acceptable. Now, let's see, we have the menu, the decor, and the invitations. Lotus, can you do the guest list?"

"Oh, yes, yes!" Lotus was again bouncing with excitement and enthusiasm. Lizzie gave what seemed to pass for a nod of approval and disappeared into the kitchen again. "We can work on the list now," Lotus said. "Let's go to the library where there's pen and paper."

They started for the library but paused at the sound of a distant heartbeat. "The helicopter," Jane said.

Lotus nodded as the *wop, wop, wop* grew more distinct. "They'll land in that field over there. Come on, we can see them from that window."

Jane followed Lotus and Hillary. She felt like a character from an old war movie about to be rescued from enemy territory.

She watched as the helicopter settled like an awkward bird onto the open, grassy field. It remained poised that way for a few moments, with the rotor blades slicing a precise circle in the heavy, moist air. The craft wobbled slightly as the blades slowed, then one side opened, and two men spilled out of the helicopter's egg-shaped belly like eager hatchlings. They ducked to avoid the turning blades and walked, in no particular hurry, toward the house.

Lotus seemed nervous. "Oh dear," she said and pulled at the beads that hung down over her ample bosom. "Oh dear, you don't suppose I'll have to talk to them, do you?"

"My guess is they'll want to talk to everyone," Jane said.

"Aunt Julia, too? Oh no, we can't allow that. It would be far to stressful for her. Can't the two of you handle it? After all, you're the ones who found him."

"Actually, Jane is the one who should talk to them," Hillary said.

"Me?" Jane couldn't keep a nervous screech out of her voice. "You're the one who found him, Hillary. If he talks to anyone, it'll be you."

Hillary had a worried look about her. "But, Jane, dear, I only found him accidentally."

Jane glared at Hillary. "Is that supposed to be a logical answer?"

Hillary gave a nervous little twittering laugh. "Why that's just the point, lamb. I never claimed to be the logical one. But you, why, you're practically a lawyer. You know all the logical answers. And for heaven's sake, what do I know? I'm just a caterer and an interior designer. And a television personality, of course. I might add, a very *good* caterer and interior designer, but—"

"Give it up, Hillary. You're in this as deep as any of us."

"I'm not." Lotus held up her pudgy hands. "I'm not in this at all."

They heard a loud knock at the front door. Lotus dropped her hands and seemed to be holding her breath. Hillary gave her hair a quick check in the mirror over the fireplace.

It was only a few seconds before Lizzie opened the wide double doors leading to the library and ushered in the two men. One of them, a tall, middle-aged man, solidly built except for a stomach that hung slightly over his belt, wore a smartly creased shirt and pants. A badge in the shape of a shield was pinned to his chest. He carried his hat in his hand. "I'm Sheriff Lonnie Harkelrode. This here's Homer Cates. He's the coroner."

Homer was a slender man of medium height. He had piercing blue eyes and dark hair that receded slightly from two sides of his forehead. A perpetual frown gave him a serious look.

There was a moment of awkward silence while the three women stared at the men. Lizzie, who now was standing behind the men, remained silent as well, but her expression was more one of scowling curiosity than of apprehension.

Finally, with a quick glance at Hillary and Lotus, Jane stepped forward and extended her hand. "Jane Ferguson," she said. She waited a moment, and when neither Lotus nor Hillary spoke, she pointed to them and said each of their names in turn. "Lotus Bean. Hillary Scarborough."

"Ferguson and Scarborough." Sheriff Harkelrode glanced at each of them. "Y'all are the ones that found the body." It was a statement rather than a question.

Hillary brought a hand to her hair. "Well, actually, I didn't—"

"Yes," Jane said, interrupting Hillary before she said something foolish that could get them in trouble. Jane couldn't imagine at the moment what that might be, but she'd learned it was always best to take precautions when it came to Hillary talking to the police.

The sheriff turned his gaze to Hillary. "You didn't what?"

"Well," Hillary turned a quick, nervous glance toward Jane, "I was just going to say that I didn't really mean to find him. Jane was the one who set out purposely to go see the body, so I'm sure—"

The sheriff turned back to Jane. "You set out purposely to find the body? How'd you know there was a body?"

Jane took a deep breath. "You see, sheriff, Hillary had already—"

"Jane is very clever about these things." Hillary had interrupted with a quick nervousness. "You see, she almost has her law degree. That's how she knows what to look for. Now, as for me, if you ever want to redecorate your house or have a party catered, you couldn't go wrong if you called me. But I know absolutely nothing about dead people."

"Uh-huh," the sheriff said, in spite of the fact that he looked confused.

"Maybe we ought to view the body," Homer said. His frown seemed to have intensified.

"Good idea." There was a slight note of relief in the sheriff's tone. He turned back to the three women. "All of you wait here. I'll be back in a little while." He turned to Lizzie. "Show us how to get to the cellar and tell everyone else in the house not to leave. I may need to question everyone."

Lotus sucked in her breath audibly at those words, but the sheriff didn't seem to hear her. He left the room with Lizzie leading the way and Homer following behind.

Lotus continued to pace the floor and twist her beads while the sheriff was gone. "I don't understand why he would want to question *me*. After all, I didn't find Uncle Bruce. What can I tell him? Oh dear, what can I possibly say to him?" She seemed near tears.

Jane did her best to calm her. "Try not to worry, Lotus. This is just standard procedure when someone has been— has died. I'm sure the sheriff will get to the bottom of it soon."

"Oh, if you could just do all the talking, and I wouldn't have to say anything." Lotus paced and twisted her beads some more. "There's going to be more of this, though. I know."

"Jane's right," Hillary said from where she had sat down on one of the horsehair sofas. "There's no need to worry. Besides, Jane will be able to answer most of the questions. My, my, just look at my nails! Jane, I do hope you can handle this quickly so I can get back and get a manicure."

Jane was staring at Lotus. "More of this? More death you mean?"

Lotus's only answer was more sobbing.

Within fifteen minutes, the sheriff was back in the library. He seemed relaxed. "Homer and the pilot are removing the body," he said. "There'll be an autopsy, of course, but preliminary exam looks like a heart attack."

"So you won't need to question us?" Lotus asked.

"Heart attack?" Jane said at the same time.

"No need for questions at this point," the sheriff said.

"Heart attack?" Jane said again.

"That's right." The sheriff put his hat back on his head. "Now, if you'll excuse me, I got to get back—"

"Wait a minute!" Jane and Hillary said at the same time. Hillary had jumped up from the sofa.

"You can't leave without us," Hillary said.

"Could I talk to you a minute?" Jane looked over her shoulder at Hillary. "Alone?"

The sheriff hesitated a moment, then shrugged. "Sure, I guess so."

Jane waved Hillary back and followed the sheriff into the hall. "What about the toe marks?" she asked when she was sure no one else could hear.

"Toe marks?"

"Where Bruce was dragged across the dirt floor in the cellar. It was pretty obvious someone dragged him to that spot to dump him so it would look like he fell, but they forgot about the toe marks."

"There aren't any toe marks down there, lady."

"Of course there are. Come on, I'll show you." Jane pulled at the sheriff's arm.

"Look here, Miz Ferguson, I don't have time for this. I got work to do back in my office." In spite of his protests, the sheriff was allowing her to lead him along.

She took him through the kitchen and out the back door to the cellar, then flipped the latch and opened the door. "They were right over there," she said as she started down the stairs.

"Right over where?" The sheriff followed close behind.

"There, see by the stairs that lead up to the . . ." Jane was shocked to see that there were, indeed, no toe marks. "They were there!" She pointed to where the marks had been. "Someone must have swept the floor. The killer!"

"Killer?" The sheriff laughed. "I think maybe you been seeing too many picture shows, Miz Ferguson. There wasn't any signs that Mr. Bean died any way 'cept by natural causes."

"There are marks on his shoes. Like someone dragged him down here."

"Marks on his shoes?" The sheriff laughed and turned to Homer. "The lady says he had marks on his shoes."

Homer snickered. The sheriff turned back to Jane. "Listen, lady, everybody out here has marks on his shoes. It's pretty rough country."

"But—"

"He threw up on himself. Drunks do that sometimes, and so do heart attack victims. Like I said, we'll wait for the autopsy."

"Sheriff, I think—"

"Tell you what. You find any more clues, you let me know." The sheriff had started up the stairs again, and Jane had the feeling he was laughing at her again.

"Wait!" Jane hurried up the stairs after him. "I was wondering if you could take Mrs. Scarborough and me back with you. In the helicopter, I mean."

The sheriff took off his hat and scratched his head. "Well, now, I would if I could, but with that body in the back, and me and Homer being the size we are, we're just about at capacity for that whirlybird. He put his hat back on and gave her a reassuring point of his finger. "Tell you what I'll do. I'll call the road department and see if we can't get that bridge fixed on a priority basis if y'all are in a hurry to get outta here."

"Priority basis? How long will that take?" Jane was frantic.

"Can't say for sure. Could be as soon as a couple of weeks."

"I can't stay here two weeks! I have to get back to my daughter."

Sheriff Harkelrode had already started out across the field toward the helicopter. The sound of the engine and of the blades slicing the air drowned out Jane's words.

9

"Two weeks? That's out of the question! I can't go that long without a manicure!" Hillary paced the floor in Jane's room where they had gone after Sheriff Harkelrode left.

Jane sat on the bed with her knees pulled up to her chin.

"And besides, I told you, we're coming up on the wedding season. It's impossible for me to be gone two weeks! And then there's my television show. We have to film next week's show on Thursday. I'm doing that segment on flower arrangements, and you have to round up all the flowers." She pointed a finger at Jane. "Fresh cut. Remember that. If we can't get them from the florist, we have to—"

"I don't want to hear about flowers and manicures and weddings or any of that!" Jane had her hands over her ears and her face buried in her knees.

"What is wrong with you, Jane? You've got to pull yourself together and get us out of this mess." Hillary stood over her with her hands on her hips.

Jane kept her head buried.

"Jane?"

She shook her head.

"Jane, talk to me."

She raised her eyes to look at Hillary. A weary gesture.

"What's the matter with you? Don't you want to get out of here?" Hillary sounded scolding.

"Everyone in this house is nuts, and one of them who's supposed to be dead won't stay in her casket, and you're asking me if I want to get out?"

Hillary sank down on the bed next to Jane, in her own weary slump. "Well, at least you sound like your old sarcastic self again," she said without much enthusiasm.

Jane curled herself into even more of a knot and didn't answer.

Hillary got up to pace again. "I can't take much more of this. You have to think of something, Jane. You have to get us out of here."

"I can't. I've exhausted all my ideas."

"No you haven't! I won't take no for an answer!"

Jane raised her eyes. "How can we leave anyway? Don't you have a wake to plan?"

"Well, there's that, but—"

"No, go ahead," Jane said with a wave of her hand. "Plan. Plan big. We've got lots of time. And since we're stuck here anyway, I'm going to find out the truth about Cassandra and Bruce."

Hillary started for the door.

"Where're you going?" Jane asked just as Hillary reached for the doorknob.

"I don't want to know any more about Cassandra than I have to know. I'm going to call Billy. He'll think of some way to get us out." She looked at her watch. "He should be back in town by now."

"Good idea, Hill," Jane said just as Hillary walked out the door. Maybe it really was a good idea, she thought. Maybe Billy could come up with something. Judging by what she'd heard Hillary say about him, he seemed to have connections with some of those in authority in the state. Maybe they were the kind of connections that could help get them rescued in considerably less than two weeks. If something didn't happen soon, she was going to have to call Jim Ed and ask him to keep Sarah a little longer—something she was loath to do, not only because she hated asking Jim Ed for anything but also because she couldn't stand the thought of being away from Sarah for more than a few days.

The possibility that Hillary's husband might be able to help lifted her spirits. She decided to go downstairs so she could hear the good news as soon as Hillary completed the call. She hoped, also, to be able to get some information from Lotus. Jane was convinced Lotus knew more about Cassandra and Bruce than she was telling. Jane had just gotten up from the bed when Hillary came rushing back into the room, her eyes wide.

"Is something wrong?" Jane asked, alarmed.

"I—I'm not sure." Hillary glanced over her shoulder, into the hall.

"What do you mean, you don't know?"

"She—she's gone."

"Who's gone?"

Hillary pointed next door.

"Cassandra? Gone? Again?" Jane felt a knot forming in her stomach. "You mean she's still not in her casket?"

Hillary shook her head. "I mean the casket's gone."

Jane moved quickly to the hallway and saw the open door leading to Cassandra's room. With Hillary close behind, she peered inside the room. It looked almost empty now that there was no longer a casket on pedestals in the middle of the floor.

"Maybe they buried her." Hillary spoke in almost a whisper.

"If they buried anything, I still say it had to be just an empty casket," Jane said.

Hillary frowned. "Why would they do such an odd thing?"

"Who knows? Nothing seems out of the ordinary for this family." Jane started for the stairway but turned back to beckon Hillary. "Come on, Hillary, you were going to call Billy, remember? And I want to try to talk to Lotus."

Lotus was just coming out of the library, her cat curled in her arm, as Jane and Hillary approached the door.

"Oh!" she said as if she was surprised to see them. "Are

you coming down to plan the party? Wake, I mean.''

"We must talk about that, Lotus." Hillary said with a wave of her hand. "But first I have to make a telephone call. I have to speak to my husband."

"Oh, well . . ." Lotus sounded disappointed. Then she added. "Your husband is playing golf."

"Nonsense," Hillary said. "He gave up golf long ago. I'm going to ask him if he can find a way to rescue us."

"Rescue you?" Lotus was genuinely puzzled.

"Oh, my!" Hillary was flustered. "It's not that we're not enjoying our stay, of course. You're very gracious. But you see, it is the wedding season, and then there's my television show. It's all about flower arrangements this time, and we simply must—"

Lotus held up one of her hands, plump as a pincushion, to stop Hillary. "It's all right. Most people don't like it out here. We're so, well, so isolated. And I suppose we've had to make our own lives in spite of our remote location. That might make us seem a bit different from other people, so I understand if you're uncomfortable and anxious to leave."

"Oh my goodness, lamb, no!" Hillary said in her most charming Southern voice. "It's not that at all, you see, it's just that I have so much to do, and—"

"Hillary!" Jane motioned with her head toward the telephone. "Call Billy, remember?"

"Oh yes, I will, I will." Hillary fluttered away to the telephone.

"When you're done with your call, we could go over the guest list," Lotus called after her. She glanced at Jane and smiled lamely.

"This wake seems awfully important to you," Jane said.

"Well, yes. I told you, it's a tradition in our family."

"Umm. I suppose you did the same thing for Cassandra before we arrived then." She was testing her, watching for a reaction.

"Cassandra?"

"Yes. I couldn't help but notice her casket isn't in the room anymore. When did you remove it? I'm surprised we didn't at least hear someone."

"Cassandra's casket?" Lotus twisted her beads in a nervous gesture.

Jane was puzzled by her attitude. "You know. In the room between my room and Hillary's."

Lotus seemed to want to avoid looking at her. "Oh yes! Yes, of course. There's to be a little family service this evening. For the burial, I mean. In the family plot. We skipped the wake. Cassie's request." Lotus put a sausage-shaped finger to her lips. "I wonder if I ought to get Cousin Chester to say a few words for her. It will mean coming here twice, of course. Once for Cassie and once for Bruce's wake. But he shouldn't mind. After all he *is* family. Maybe I should call him." She twisted her beads again. "Yes, yes. I think I should. As soon as Hillary's off the phone." She turned away, moving toward the phone, then whirled back to Jane. Her movements were quick and jerky—the movements of a nervous person. "You're welcome to come, if you'd like. To the burial service, I mean."

Jane nodded and tried to smile. She would go. It might be a chance to prove that Cassandra was not in the casket and to put an end to the crazy charade about her death.

Hillary put down the telephone and walked toward them in her finishing school gait, her expression crestfallen. "I couldn't get him. The maid said he was . . ." She gave Jane a troubled look.

"Was what, Hillary?"

"Playing golf."

Jane glanced at Lotus, then back to Hillary. "You're kidding!"

"Can we still have the party?" Lotus still looked apprehensive.

"Party?" Hillary gave her a questioning look.

"Wake, I mean. For Bruce. You haven't forgotten already, have you? We're going to do it along with America Elizabeth's birthday party, remember? After all, that's what we hired you for." Lotus's tone was soft but pressing.

"Oh, the wake. Yes, of course. We must start our planning right away. I'll have to leave, of course, to go back to Prosper, because I'm certain I can get Billy to fix the bridge, but I can always come back later to help set things up for you.''

Lotus's face brightened. ''Wonderful! We can start working on the plans as soon as I make this phone call.'' She moved toward the phone, her hips rolling beneath her loose skirt like ships riding the crests of waves.

''Who's she calling?'' Hillary asked.

''Chester, the patron saint of hands in the till. Seems you were right. They're going to have a quickie funeral for Cassandra. Out at the graveyard, and they want him to do the honors. He'll be here for Cassandra's funeral and Bruce's wake as well.''

Hillary looked troubled. ''They're going to bury her? Not just an empty casket? Does that mean she's really *dead?* And what we've been seeing is really a ghost after all?

''I don't think so, Hillary, but none of it makes sense. I'm going to that funeral so I can ask some questions and get to the bottom of this. I hope you're right about Chester. I hope he can give us some insight.''

Hillary seemed alarmed. ''What am I going to do? I can't wear this! She looked down at her wrinkled silk slacks. ''It's the wrong color for a funeral and not nearly dressy enough.''

''You don't have to go, Hillary.''

''But surely I'm invited.''

''I don't know. I suppose, but it's not exactly the party of the year. I'm sure you can think of better things to do.''

Hillary seemed to have not heard Jane. She wore a pensive expression. ''Let's see. There's sure to be a reception afterward. I could do a nice cold chicken dish with rosemary and lemon, and those lovely strawberries in the beds in back would be perfect in little meringue shells with—''

''It's just the family, Hillary. Lotus didn't mention a reception. Why don't you just concentrate on the wake for Bruce?''

''Really, Jane! I don't know how you do things in California, but in the South, we take death very seriously. There's such a thing as tradition and ritual, you know.''

''Oh yeah, the South is just full of it.''

Hillary turned away from Jane and started back into the library. "I'm not even going to ask you what you mean by that remark, Jane, because I don't want to have to fire you again. At least not until after you've helped produce that show we have to shoot on Thursday."

"And the wedding season. Don't forget that," Jane called after her.

"Don't press your luck, Jane. I have done dozens of weddings without you."

"Is that a threat, Hillary?"

There was no response from Hillary. She simply turned away and spoke to Lotus. "Let's have another look at the parlor so I can suggest how to arrange the serving tables."

When Hillary and Lotus left the room, Jane browsed the shelves of the Bean family library with more restlessness than interest. Most of the books were novels from past decades and held little appeal for her. She couldn't stop thinking about the toe marks in the basement floor and about Cassandra not staying in her casket.

It would be a great comfort to her, she thought, to talk to someone who was neither crazy nor eccentric about all of that. Someone normal. Someone like Beau Jackson. She debated with herself about whether or not she should call him again. The last thing she wanted was to appear frightened or helpless. And anyway, it didn't pay to become too dependent on anyone. She'd learned that lesson with Jim Ed.

The clock on the mantel struck five times with a sad, eerie chime. Jane could hear the muffled sound of Hillary's and Lotus's voices in the parlor. When was the funeral? she wondered. It would have to be soon, since it would be getting dark shortly. Maybe they were waiting for Chester to arrive. In any event, Lotus didn't seem to be in any hurry to give up her party planning.

Jane glanced at the telephone again, then at the faded daylight oozing through the window. Depressing. Everything about the Beans' house was depressing. She was going to lose her mind if she couldn't speak to someone on the outside soon. Maybe she should just call Jim Ed's place and ask to speak to Sarah. That would cheer her up.

She reached for the telephone and dialed his number in Birmingham along with the code and number for her credit card. In a little while, a female voice answered the phone.

"Ferguson residence." It didn't sound much like Miss Alabama.

"Leslie Ann?" she said, just to make sure.

"No, I'm sorry, Miss Leslie has gone out for the evening."

"Who is this?"

"I'm the maid. Shall I take a message?"

"The maid. Oh, of course." There hadn't been money for a maid when she was married to Jim Ed. Not even a once-a-week cleaning woman. There'd barely been money to pay the rent in their small apartment while he was in law school and she was working to keep him there. But of course she didn't have a rich daddy with his own law firm to make Jim Ed a partner the way Leslie Ann did. "Uh, could I speak to Sarah?" she finally managed to say.

"Miss Sarah is out with her parents. They've gone to dinner in the Galleria and then to Planet Fun. May I ask who's calling?"

Anger jabbed at Jane's innards with a hot poker. Her parents! This woman had her nerve referring to skinny Miss Alabama as Sarah's parent! "This is Sarah's *mother*." She spat the words out with searing indignation.

"Her mother?"

"Jane Ferguson. Her mother." Her anger was giving way to an irrational uneasy feeling that maybe everyone, even Sarah, had forgotten her in the two days they'd been separated.

"Oh yes, of course. I beg your pardon," the oh-so-efficient voice on the other end of the line said. "When the family returns, I'll tell Miss Sarah you called. Good night."

"Wait! Is she—" The dial tone whined in her ear. "Is she all right?" she said weakly to the empty sound. She hung up the phone in a darkness that had nothing to do with the dying light of day.

The *family?* Her *parents?* Jane felt as if she had somehow been written out of a script that was supposed to be her life. To save herself from despair, she reached for the phone again and dialed Beau Jackson's number.

The telephone rang several times before Jane heard the receiver click. Something inside her quickened with hope only to die again when she realized that the click was nothing more than the answering machine and Beau's voice telling her once again that he was unable to come to the phone and would she please leave a message.

"Beau, this is Jane." Even as she spoke the words, she wished she had just hung up, because now she didn't know what to say without sounding as if she was as loony as everyone else in the house. But now that she had started, she had to say something that would make sense. "I'll call back later when I—"

"Jane?" It was Beau's voice. He had picked up the phone and interrupted her message.

"Beau?"

"Where are you? I've been trying to call you for two days."

Jane was surprised at how glad she was to hear his voice. "I'm with Hillary. We're marooned out here in Taladega County. The storm washed out a bridge."

"Washed out a bridge? What bridge?"

"I don't think the bridge has a name. It crosses Sycamore Creek, and it's on a little dirt road leading up to a house owned by a family called the Beans."

"The Beans? The Beans of Taladega County?"

"Yes, do you know them?"

Beau laughed. "Oh, yeah. Everybody knows the Beans. You know that horoscope column that runs in the paper every day? One of 'em writes that. Cassandra Bean."

"Cassandra is dead, according to her family members, anyway."

"She's what?"

"Dead. Only, well . . ." Jane looked over her shoulder to make sure no one was listening, then cupped her hand over the receiver to keep her words from being overheard.

"Only, for a dead woman, she spends a lot of time out of her casket."

"What did you say? I think we have a bad connection."

"I said she won't stay in her casket." Jane articulated the words carefully, one by one.

There was a long silence, then, "Jane, are you all right?"

"Yes. I mean, no. I'm trapped in a house with a bunch of loonies and the walking dead. Listen to me, Beau. I know one of them really did die. Uncle Bruce. And I think someone killed him."

"Listen, hon, have you called the sheriff out there in Taladega County? His name is Harkelrode."

"Of course I called him. He said it was natural causes, a heart attack, but I believe he may have been murdered. Harkelrode wouldn't believe me."

"Uh-huh." Beau sounded worried.

"And you don't either, do you?"

"I didn't say that, Jane. I, uh—listen, I know how remote it is out there and sometimes it starts to get to you. Especially a city girl."

"Don't patronize me, Beau Jackson!"

"Jane, I don't mean to patronize. It's just that—"

"I'm sorry I called and bothered you. Good-bye."

She was about to hang up the phone when she heard his voice. Urgent. "Wait! Don't hang up!"

"What?" She made no attempt to hide her irritation.

"I'm sorry. What can I say?" His penitence sounded genuine. "It's just that, well, you don't sound like yourself."

"Of course I don't sound like myself! I am stuck out here in La-La Land!" Her words blasted the receiver like rocks, hardened by stress.

"That's just my point. I think you've been there with those people so long you're beginning to—"

"Why didn't you ask me why I thought Bruce was murdered? Why do you just assume I've become one of the loonies, too?" She sounded angry. Maybe even petulant. She hadn't meant to sound that way. She wished now she could take the words back so she could remold them to sound cool and intelligent.

"All right, tell me. Why do you think this man was murdered?" Very cool and intelligent.

Was he being patronizing again? Or just trying to make amends? It didn't matter anyway, because she was still edgy. "Because of the toe marks." The words were clipped. Almost angry sounding.

"The what?"

"Toe marks." She told him, then, how she and Hillary had seen the toe marks in the dirt floor. How that must have meant Bruce had been dragged to the cellar and how the marks had disappeared by the time the sheriff went down to investigate.

His only response was a detached sounding, "Uh-huh." It was that tone that kept her from trying to explain further about Cassandra and her sometimes empty casket. She was wishing more and more now that she hadn't called him at all. "Jane? Are you still there?" he said after a long silence.

"Yes." The edge to her voice was becoming more jagged.

"This is all real interesting." He used the Southern pronunciation: INA-restin'.

"Yeah, I'm sure."

"I'm going to, uh . . . Well, for one thing, I'm going to see what I can do about that bridge."

"You do that, Beau."

"I don't want to worry you or anything, but there's some guy escaped from the state pen."

"I heard."

"You hang in there, hon, you hear?" He always said "heah."

She almost told him not to call her hon, but all she said was, "Yeah, sure." Then she hung up before he made her feel even more foolish.

She had just turned away from the telephone when Lotus and Hillary entered the library. They had come to find a cookbook Lotus said she was sure was on one of those shelves. They had just begun searching for it when Lizzie opened the two double doors leading into the room from the hallway.

"The minister is here," she announced.

"The minister? Oh, my goodness, I've let the time get away," Lotus said. "The family is probably already assembled out at the plot. Tell Cousin Chester I'll be right there."

" 'Tis not Cousin Chester. 'Tis another one." Lizzie spoke, as always, without changing her facial expression.

"Another one? How can that be? I called Cousin Chester myself."

"Chester is confined to his bed in his mother's house with a cold. He sent a replacement."

"Oh dear!" Lotus sounded perplexed. "I told you helicopters interfere with the vibes."

Lizzie turned around to look behind her and then moved aside for the minister to enter.

Jane gasped when she saw him. The man who stepped into the library wearing a clerical collar was the same man who had been at the gas station and who had come to repair the telephone.

10

Lotus seemed in a hurry to get the minister out of the room. "Excuse us, please," she said over her shoulder to Jane and Hillary as she pulled the man along with her. "I have to go over some things with the preacher. We'll do some more work on the party later."

"Have we met before?" Hillary said. She was trying to see around Lotus to get a better view of the man.

Lotus answered for him quickly. "Oh, no. He's not from Prosper like Cousin Chester. He's from—somewhere else."

"Well he certainly looks . . ." Lotus was gone, hurrying the minister toward the back of the house.

". . . familiar," Hillary said after Lotus and the minister had disappeared. She turned to Jane. "Doesn't he look familiar to you?"

"Of course he does." There was an urgency in Jane's tone. "He's the same man we saw at the gas station and the same man who was supposed to be fixing the telephone."

"The gas station. Why, of course! That's where I saw him." Hillary frowned. "But why would a minister be working in a gas station?"

"Because he's not a minister."

"Of course he's a minister. He was wearing a collar." Hillary frowned at what she apparently thought was Jane's obtuseness.

"He's not a minister." Jane was emphatic. "And he's not a gas station attendant or a telephone repairman."

Hillary shook her head. "I don't understand. If he's none of those, then who is he?"

"An escaped convict!"

Hillary sucked in her breath and put one of her hands to her mouth. "Escaped convict! How can you tell?"

"Well, of course I can't tell for sure, but it makes sense, doesn't it? The sheriff said the man who escaped from prison was thought to be heading in this direction. This guy keeps showing up in different disguises. So what else are we supposed to think?"

Hillary looked puzzled. "But didn't the sheriff say somebody had seen the man in Birmingham?"

Jane shook her head. "He said someone *thought* they spotted him in Birmingham. The point is, he's still on the loose, so no one knows where he is."

Hillary glanced nervously toward the doorway through which Lotus and the man had gone. "Do you think we should warn Lotus?"

"I think Lotus already knows. Didn't you see how strangely she was acting?"

Hillary's brow wrinkled as if she was considering what Jane just said. "Well, yes, but she *is* a little bit strange, anyway, don't you think?"

Jane rolled her eyes. "Oh, you noticed, did you?"

Hillary was still pondering what Jane had said. "If she knows that man is the escaped convict, why doesn't she call the sheriff?"

"Because I think she's helping him for some reason."

"But why?"

"I don't know. Maybe he's her lover or something. Maybe he has something to do with Bruce's death and Cassandra's antics. I can only guess."

Hillary, the pensive frown still on her brow, nodded her head. "I see, so Lotus is probably not in danger then." Her

eyes widened as realization came to her. "But we could
be. If she thinks we know."

Jane nodded. "Now you're catching on."

"What are we going to do? Should we tell the sheriff?"

"I don't know." Jane glanced at the phone. "I'm not
sure he'd believe us. He doesn't seem inclined to believe
anything we tell him."

"Oh dear." Hillary put her fingertips to her forehead and
closed her eyes as if she had a headache. "I'm not used to
having my credibility doubted. If that starts to erode . . .
My Lord, I can't even think about it. I mean no one would
watch a television show on how to make bouillabaisse from
someone they can't trust."

Jane felt momentarily disoriented. "Bouillabaisse?"

"Didn't I tell you? That's what we're doing for the show
the week after next. I wanted to give you some time to
think about the fish."

"You want me to think about *fish?*"

"Why, yes." Hillary gave an authoritative toss of her
head. "We can't always get the Mediterranean varieties in
Prosper, so you may have to substitute—"

"Hillary, how do you *do* this?" Jane put her hands to
her head. "How do you get me talking about things like
fish?"

Hillary managed to appear both defensive and haughty
at the same time. "All I said was—"

"I know, I know!" Jane held up a hand to ward off any
more from Hillary. "Forget it, Hillary." She started for the
door. "I'm going to that funeral."

Hillary nodded. "If you're going to be doing more investigating, I suppose I ought to go with you. I've gotten
rather good at that. Investigating, I mean."

Jane chose not to argue with her. At least it was better
than talking about fish.

The family group was subdued. Only Julia cried openly
as Winston, his head down, kept his arm around her. Katrin
seemed to wipe a tear from her eye. Lizzie, her mouth a
thin, white line, showed no more emotion than the old
gravestones.

The minister got all the way through the eulogy and then the prayers at the end of the service without a hitch. Jane was beginning to doubt her suspicion of him. He sounded professional, as if he'd been conducting the rituals of the church for years.

Finally, after he had pronounced the last amen, he looked at the family and, wearing what seemed to be a pious, compassionate expression, said, "Your cousin Chester Collins sends his regrets that he could not conduct this service. Since I was also visiting the family and since I am a minister of the word of God, he asked me to speak in his stead. I hope I have served you well, and may God's blessings rest upon all of you." He walked away from the little group, across the bleak expanse of ancient grave markers, some tilting sideways crazily toward the earth, others already fallen like a battalion of defeated soldiers.

Jane felt uncertain about what to do for a moment, but eventually, with a determined glance in Hillary's direction, she ran to follow the minister and called to him.

"Excuse me! Reverend, just a minute, please."

The man turned back to look at her.

"Haven't I seen you somewhere before?" Jane said, hurrying to catch up with him. Hillary was close behind her.

"You've been to my church in Birmingham?"

"Birmingham? No. I mean . . ." She decided to be direct. "You were here repairing the telephone, and I saw you in the gas station, too. Only you weren't in a clerical collar. I was just wondering if you could explain that."

"I beg your pardon?"

"I *have* seen you before. I'm sure of it." Jane was beginning to feel extremely nervous. If he truly was an escaped convict hiding in a number of disguises, then she had just put herself in danger.

The minister chuckled softly. "You would be surprised at how often that happens to me, my child. People thinking they've seen me somewhere else. I'm afraid I just have a very ordinary face." With that, he turned again and walked away.

"You certainly don't know much about repairing telephone wires," Hillary called to him.

He turned around again. "Repairing telephone wires?" He seemed puzzled for a moment, then he chuckled. "You're right about that. I don't know a thing about it. I just try to keep a direct line open to God."

Jane watched him leave, feeling both embarrassed and confused.

"He's lying," Hillary said.

"Yes." Jane nodded her head, still watching him. "He is."

"He's the escaped prisoner, and he must have killed Bruce. Lotus may have even helped him." Hillary crossed her arms in a confident, satisfied manner.

"Why did he kill Bruce and no one else?" Jane asked.

"Because Bruce discovered the truth about him. That he's an escaped convict." Hillary gave her the kind of look she might give a particularly slow child. "My goodness, Jane, you've been to law school. You should be able to figure out these things. And didn't I tell you, I am getting rather good at this?"

"You told me, Hill, but one thing that occurs to me is that if he killed Bruce because he figured out who he is, will we be next? I mean, when I confronted him about the gas station attendant and the telephone repairman, he must have figured out we're on to him. And you've already drawn your own conclusion about what that means."

Hillary's eyes widened, and she grew pale. "Oh my Lord! You should have kept your mouth shut, Jane. You never should have confronted him about that."

"*I* shouldn't have confronted him? How about Miss Private Investigator telling him he didn't know how to repair a telephone?"

Hillary seemed stunned for a moment before she spoke again. "How do you keep getting me into these situations, Jane? What is it about you that attracts trouble?"

"What do you mean, I attract . . ." Hillary was walking away from her, going back toward the house where the family had already gone. Jane sighed and followed her.

Dinner, they discovered when they got back into the house, was cold sandwiches served from the buffet. None of the family members spoke much as they picked up their sandwiches, and none of them stayed in the dining room to eat. Jane was disappointed. It might have been an opportunity to ask more questions. Since there was nothing else to do, she and Hillary took their meals upstairs as well.

Hillary followed Jane into her room. "I think we should push the bureau up against the door tonight," she said. She set her sandwich down and went to the bureau and gave it a push to test the heaviness.

Jane watched her but didn't speak. She assumed that meant Hillary would be in her room again tonight. She sat down in the chair next to the window and nibbled at her sandwich.

"What are we going to do, Jane?" Hillary was still standing by the bureau, and she looked worried.

"Did you call Billy again? Did you ask him to get someone out to repair the bridge?"

"I tried. Still didn't get him. Just the maid telling me he was still playing golf. I declare, Jane. How long can a person play golf?"

"Maybe Beau can do something. I told him about the bridge."

"*Someone* has to do *something!* I have never in my life worn anything two days in a row, much less three! I'm going to be forced to wear that dress Lotus loaned me again, and it's not appropriate for day wear!" She sounded near tears.

Jane only half heard her, though. She was looking down at the front of the house. "He's leaving," she said. "Maybe we won't have to worry about moving the bureau."

"What? Who's leaving?"

"The minister. Or telephone man. Whoever. He's leaving. See? He just got in that car."

Hillary hurried to the window in time to see a dark sedan pull out of the driveway. "But he's trapped here on this side of the bridge, just like we are. He could easily come back."

Jane knew what Hillary had said was true. She would be
ery glad to have someone in the room with her tonight
nd to have that bureau shoved against the door.

She continued to watch the car as it disappeared from
ight along the road that led away from the bridge. Hillary
tood beside her, watching, too. Both had forgotten about
heir cold supper.

While they stood there, Jane caught a glimpse of some-
hing white near the corner of the house. Hillary must have
een it, too, because she sucked in her breath. Jane and
Iillary looked at each other, neither of them speaking at
irst, then Hillary whispered, ''What was that?''

Jane shook her head and shrugged slightly.

''It was her, wasn't it? Cassandra?'' Hillary was still
vhispering.

Jane started to deny it, to say that it must have been a
eflection caused by a lamp being lit somewhere in the
ouse, but before the words were out of her mouth, she saw
t again: a woman in white, moving like an apparition to-
vard the family cemetery.

Hillary had seen it, too. ''Oh my Lord, Jane! She won't
ven stay in the grave.''

Jane turned away from the window and started for the
oor. ''She was never in the grave to start with, Hillary. I
old you that woman's not dead. I just can't figure out why
veryone is pretending she is. I'm going down there.''

''You're what?'' Hillary's voice was high-pitched and
creeching.

''I'm going to find out what this is all about.'' Jane
pened the door.

Hillary ran after her. ''Wait for me! You're not leaving
ne here alone.''

Jane allowed Hillary to catch up with her, then they both
aced down the hall and down the front staircase. Not a
ingle family member was to be seen as they crossed the
ntry hall. Jane pulled open the heavy front door and
tepped outside with Hillary at her side. As the door closed
ehind them, Jane hesitated a moment, thinking she must
e crazy to be chasing after someone in the dark when there

was supposed to be an escaped convict roaming around
But Hillary's cry, "There she is!" distracted her from her
moment of common sense.

Together they ran after the figure, which still was moving
toward the cemetery. Once they reached the edge of the
graveyard, Jane lost sight of the figure, but the gate was
still open, so she passed through the opening and stood just
inside, looking around.

"Do you see her?" Hillary asked, hovering nearby.

"No, but I'm sure she ran in here."

"I think we should go back." Hillary's voice sounded
shaky.

"You're probably right," Jane said, but instead of turning around, she took a step farther into the cemetery.

"Jane . . ."

"She—it—whoever it was has to be in here somewhere." Jane kept walking, moving ever closer to the new
grave.

"That's just what I'm afraid—ow!"

Jane turned around to see that Hillary had stumbled over
one of the fallen gravestones. She stood beside it, rubbing
her leg. "Are you all right?" Jane asked in a whisper.

"All right? You're asking me if I'm all right? My leg is
throbbing, and I'm scared out of my wits. Of course I'm
not all right!" Hillary's tone had taken on a note of hys-
teria.

"Just stay where you are. I'll be back in a minute." Jane
moved away, picking her way through the gravestones.

Within seconds, Hillary was next to her.

When they reached the new grave, Jane still had not seen
the figure again. It was becoming difficult to see in the
growing darkness, but the white garment the figure had on
would be easy to spot.

She stopped when they got to the new grave and looked
around. Still nothing. The grave, she noticed, had been
filled. A fresh mound of dirt covered it now, rounded off
like a cathedral dome.

"Where do you suppose she went?" Hillary's voice was

still trembling. "I mean, you don't think she, you know, went back into the grave, do you?"

"Of course not," Jane said, looking around. "She, or whoever that was, must not have come in here, she must have . . ." Jane stopped speaking when she saw headlights through the lattice ironwork of the gate. A car had driven up the road that wound along the side of the house toward the neighbors, who were several miles away—the same road on which the minister had driven away. Now the car was stopped.

"What is it?" Hillary asked.

"That car." She heard the solid thud of a door closing, but the headlights blinded her from seeing what had happened. Then the car backed up, turned around, and disappeared. "I think someone got inside."

"Someone? Who? What does that mean?"

"I don't know what it means. Maybe it means our ghost has a chauffeur."

"What . . ."

"Come on." Jane hurried toward the gate. "Let's see if we can make out where the car is going."

Hillary once again followed closely as they moved as quickly as possible through the maze of tombstones. "Oh my Lord! Look!" Hillary was pointing toward the gate.

Jane turned to look and, now that they were closer, saw what Hillary had seen. The gate was closed. Jane leapt over the few remaining tombstones between her and the gate and tried to push it open. It wouldn't budge. The gate was locked. She glanced around at the high walls, trying to hold back panic. The walls were too high to scale. She pushed at the gate again, but to no avail. She and Hillary were trapped in the cemetery.

11

"Do something, Jane! Get us out of here!"

It was difficult to see Hillary in the darkness, but her voice sounded frightened.

"What can I do? I'd have to be a lizard to scale these walls." Jane knew she wasn't doing a very good job of keeping fear out of her own voice.

"Well there has to be some way out of here. We can't just—oooh!"

"What's wrong, Hill?" Jane tried to see into the night, which was becoming steadily darker as rain began to fall in a soft mist. Hillary was nowhere in sight. "Hillary? Hillary, where are you?"

"I'm here!" came a muffled answer.

"Where?" Jane was feeling her way through the darkness, hands in front of her, like a blind person. Even the moon and stars were hiding in the blackness.

"Here. On the ground."

"On the ground?"

"I fell."

Jane felt a moment of near panic. A surge of adrenaline made her head pound. "For heaven's sake, Hillary, are you all right?"

"I think I broke a nail."

"Good Lord, Hillary!" She was still trying to move toward Hillary's voice when she stumbled over something and almost fell herself.

"Ow!"

"Is that you, Hill?"

"Yes. You just bumped into me."

"Sorry, but it's dark as hell out here," Jane said.

Hillary was trying to pick herself up. "I'm getting wet! Jane, we've got to get out of here. These silk slacks aren't supposed to get wet. They have to be dry cleaned."

"Geez, if I'd known you were worried about your slacks, I'd have had us out of here long ago."

"Jane, I hate it when you get that way. Do you know what these slacks cost?"

The rain had increased from a mist to a steady downpour, and Jane could hear Hillary slapping at her wet pant legs in a futile gesture.

"Come on," Jane said, feeling around in the darkness for Hillary's hand. "I think I remember a tool shed over there by the wall where it runs next to the road. "We can duck in there until it stops raining."

She found Hillary's hand, and together, the two of them made their way, stumbling toward the wall. As they got closer, Jane could make out a hulking shape that seemed to be hugging the wall. That had to be the tool shed. She led Hillary toward it.

Feeling along the rough plank wall of the shed until she found the door, Jane turned the knob and was relieved to find that it wasn't locked. It was hot and musty inside the shed, but at least it was dry.

"Is there a light?" Hillary asked.

"I don't know." Jane was waving her hands above her head, searching for a string to pull a light on when she remembered there wasn't any electricity anyway. Hillary, she sensed, was feeling along the shelving on the wall. Suddenly Jane heard a screech, like someone screaming, followed by a plaintive moan. The sound was coming from somewhere nearby, somewhere inside the graveyard.

"What was that?" Hillary was suddenly beside her, gripping her arm.

"I don't know," Jane whispered. Fright had stolen her voice. "An animal maybe. Or a bird."

Hillary edged closer. "Or one of the—you know—residents."

"Residents?"

Hillary gripped her arm tighter, her long nails digging into Jane's flesh. "You know, residents of the graveyard."

"For Christ's sake, Hillary, dead people don't make noises."

The sound came again. A screech followed by a moan.

Jane and Hillary both screamed and hugged each other for comfort. Both were too frightened to speak for a moment. Jane could feel her heart pummeling the walls of her chest.

"They don't like us here in their neighborhood," Hillary whispered. "You've got to get us out!"

"Believe me, Hillary, I would if I knew how." The wind had come up suddenly, like a thief, and rattled the door to the shed, almost drowning out Jane's words.

Hillary sniffed and then sniffed again.

"Are you crying, Hillary?"

Hillary pulled away from Jane and turned her back to her, crying harder. "This is not the way I planned to go. I mean, not when I'm young and not at the hands of some ghost. Certainly not in wrinkled silk."

"Aw, come on, Hillary, don't do that. Cheer up. I'm sure that when it's your time to go, you'll do it in style, with your hair perfect and your nails done and in some designer outfit that's just been freshly pressed."

Hillary sniffed again, then turned back to Jane. "You think so?"

"I'm sure of it."

"That would be so wonderful. I mean, I'm such a mess right now. I would be so embarrassed if I were found dead like this."

"Of course you would."

There was a moment of silence, then, "Jane . . ."

"Yes, Hillary."

"It didn't work."

"What do you mean?"

"I am not in the least comforted. There is a ghost out there, and it is trying to get us."

"Nonsense, Hillary, I told you it's just—"

The wind threw itself at the tiny building in a gust, screaming as it tore itself around the corners and pushing the door open in a sudden clattering burst. At the same moment, the scream became louder and something entered the building with them.

"Jane!" Hillary's voice was an urgent, frightened whisper. "There's something in here."

"Nonsense," Jane whispered back to her, in spite of the fact that she knew it wasn't nonsense. Something *had* entered the shed. At that very moment, she heard a thump and something fell off of one of the shelves.

Hillary screamed and grabbed Jane, pinning her arms to her sides. Her scream was answered by a high-pitched screech. It was a screech Jane recognized.

"Hillary! Hillary, it's OK. It's just Hieronymus."

"Hieronymus? The cat?"

"Yes, the cat."

"Are you sure?"

Her question was answered by a plaintive meow.

"What's she doing out here in the rain? Cats don't like to get wet." Hillary's disembodied voice came out of the darkness.

"That's why she ran into the shed. To get out of the rain. And that scream we heard. It must have been Hieronymus. Cats sound that way sometimes." Jane felt the cat curling herself around her ankles, seeking warmth and attention.

"Cats in graveyards. That's a bad sign." Hillary was still sticking close to her.

"Why do you say that?" Jane stooped to pick up Hieronymus and was holding her in her arms, stroking her.

"They can harbor the souls of the dead."

"For crying out loud, Hillary, where do you come up with stuff like that?"

"I don't know. It just comes to me. And I'll tell you something else. This place is really scary. Really dark and scary."

"Thanks for sharing that, Hillary."

There was no response from Hillary, and in the long silence that followed, Jane began to regret her sarcastic remark.

"Hill . . . Hill, where are you?"

Again there was no response, but she heard a shuffling at the opposite end of the tiny shed.

"Don't be upset, Hillary. We'll be all right, you'll see. Nothing is going to happen to us out here, and someone will let us out in the morning."

Hillary's response was an ear-piercing scream, at the same time a light briefly illuminated the shed's one window. The sound and the sudden light startled Jane, and she dropped Hieronymus, who meowed again, this time with anger, as she hit the floor.

"What was—"

"A face! A face!" Hillary interrupted Jane, still screaming.

"What face? Where?"

"In the window! There! I saw it!" Hillary's voice was choked with fear. "It was—unearthly."

"Hillary, calm down, please. I'm sure there's some logical explanation."

"No, it was her. It was her." Hillary was still nearly hysterical.

"Who, Hillary?" Jane did her best to keep her voice calm, hoping to have a calming effect on Hillary."

"Her. America Elizabeth! She looked just like the painting Lotus was doing."

"America Elizabeth? But she's—"

"I know, I know. Don't say it."

"Come on now, Hill." Jane groped in the dark, trying to find Hillary's hand to hold in the hope that she could comfort her. "You're just upset."

"Of course I'm upset. It was America Elizabeth! With a shawl over her head, just like the painting." She sounded as if she was near tears.

"Hill . . ."

"It was America Elizabeth."

"OK, OK," Jane said. She had found Hillary's hand again and was holding it with both of hers, trying to comfort her.

"Oh my Lord!" Hillary said.

"What?"

"There she is. See?" Jane could sense Hillary pointing to the window. She moved closer and peered outside. There was a dim light just outside, like a flashlight maybe, or a lantern, its light diffused by the rain. Someone was carrying the light. Someone walking through the graveyard. Someone wearing a long dress and a shawl draped over her head.

"Oh my God!" Jane said under her breath.

"It's the ghost of America Elizabeth!" Hillary was almost squeaking. "They said she roams around, didn't they? It's her. I know it! I just know it!"

"There just has to be some logical explanation." Jane felt she was trying to convince herself as much as she was trying to convince Hillary.

"You have to admit it looks like her." That frightened squeak was still there in Hillary's voice.

"It does. It looks like her." Jane knew she sounded worried.

"It's her!"

"She."

"What?"

"It's *she.*"

"Oh my Lord, so you admit it!"

"Forget it, Hillary."

"How can I forget it? There's a ghost out there. You saw her yourself."

Jane took a deep breath. "Look, Hillary, we've both got to be calm about this."

"But you admitted you saw—"

"I saw something, OK? I don't know what—I mean

who. But whoever it was obviously doesn't want to do us any harm.''

"How do you know that?"

"She's walking away, isn't she? If she wanted to do us harm, she'd be in here attacking us.''

"Maybe she's gone to get reinforcements. More of the walking dead." Hillary was whispering again.

"For Christ's sake, Hillary, will you stop it?"

"I can't die like this, Jane, I just can't. My nails!" She had begun to sob. "Jane, I can't bear to even look at my hands!"

"Try not to worry, Hillary. We'll get you a manicure in no time at all."

There was a moment of silence. Hillary had even stopped her sobbing. "Are you being sarcastic again?"

"No! No, Hillary, I mean it. I do."

"I can't see you. Are you laughing?"

"Of course not."

"It's not good that one's last moments should be spent in mockery."

"Hillary, will you just stop it!"

There was another sob. "I'm just so tired."

"I know. So am I. Why don't we sit down over there on the floor opposite the window and try to rest." Jane was trying to make her way to Hillary again.

"We don't know what we'll be sitting on." Hillary said.

"Try not to think about it."

"Oh *that's* comforting."

"Are you being sarcastic, Hillary?"

"There is not a sarcastic bone in my body!" Hillary spoke in her most indignant Southern belle voice.

Jane finally coaxed Hillary into sitting down on the floor with her. They sat with their backs leaning against the wall, listening to the wind and the rain with Hieronymus curled in a spiral next to Jane. In a little while, Jane heard Hillary's now-familiar soft snore and felt her head fall onto her shoulder. Jane hadn't realized that she had slept at all until she was startled awake by the sound of pounding on the door.

She opened her eyes, disoriented for a moment, looking at the unfamiliar surroundings. The blue-gray light of morning had crept into the window of the tiny shed. There was nothing in the shed with them except a few gardening tools, evidently used to keep up the cemetery. It looked oddly benign, especially after the harrowing night they'd just spent. Hieronymus had her eye on a spider spinning a web in the corner.

The pounding on the door continued.

Hillary sat up straight. "What's that?"

"Are you in there?" a female voice from the outside called.

Jane reached for the door.

"Don't!" Hillary said.

Jane gave her a questioning look, her hand on the door.

Hillary's eyes were wide with fear. "It could be—you know—her. America Elizabeth!"

"Ms. Ferguson! Ms. Scarborough, are you in there?"

"Katrin!" Jane said and opened the door. Just as she did, the cat rushed out and skimmed across the graveyard, darting between gravestones.

Katrin was dressed in jeans, a faded shirt, and a straw hat. She stepped into the shed. "What are y'all doing out here?" Her eyes took in the two of them. "My Lord, you look like a couple of drowned rats."

The little cry that came from Hillary sounded as if she was in pain, and she brushed, furtively, at her silk slacks again.

"Thank God you found us," Jane said, "we've been here all night."

"All night?" Katrin seemed shocked. "But why? We gave you perfectly good beds to sleep in."

"We got trapped here, that's why." Hillary was frantic. "The gate was locked, and we couldn't get out."

Katrin's puzzled frown deepened. "The gate was locked? You mean after the service yesterday? You've been here all that time?"

"Not exactly," Jane said. "You see, we thought we saw—well, we came out here to look at something, and—"

"We saw a ghost," Hillary blurted.

Katrin gave a dismissive wave of her hand, along with a "Psss." She shook her head. "People are always seeing ghosts around here. America Elizabeth, especially."

"Yes!" Hillary was screeching again. "That's who it was! America Elizabeth!"

"Look, we're not sure who or what we saw," Jane said, "but the fact is, when we came out here to investigate, the gate somehow got closed and locked, and we were forced to spend the night here. We came in here to get out of the rain."

Katrin shook her head. "Well, you'd better get yourselves cleaned up and get to breakfast. Aunt Lizzie doesn't like it when people don't show up. I guess you're lucky I decided to do some gardening out here this morning. I saw you through the window when I walked over here to get the hoe."

"You're a gardener?" There was still a slight tremble to Hillary's voice, but at least the screech was gone.

Katrin gave a dry laugh. "That's what Winston calls me."

"I take it you don't like that title," Jane said as she tried to get a reluctant Hillary to step out of the shed and into the graveyard.

"I'm a plant biologist."

"Oh my!" There was a note of admiration in Hillary's exclamation.

"And all these herbicides"—she pointed to the shelves lining the walls of the shed—"they're not my idea." She sounded defensive.

"Well, of course not," Hillary said. She seemed, for the moment, to have forgotten about both her wrinkled slacks and America Elizabeth.

"The hoe works just fine for all this *Digitalis purpurea,*" Katrin said, with a definitive shake of her head.

"All this what?" Hillary's brow wrinkled in a puzzled expression.

"Foxglove."

"Oh, of course. I knew that." Hillary smiled. "They can

be unruly, but they're really quite nice for informal gardens. One of the more prolific perennials.''

"It's not really a perennial, you know. It's a biennial." Katrin's face had lit up. This was obviously something she enjoyed discussing.

"Well, yes," Hillary agreed, "but once it's established, it perennializes itself. You know, self-seeding."

"True," Katrin said. "Are you familiar with the variety called Shirley? It can grow up to five feet tall."

Hillary launched into a description of how she had used several varieties in a garden she had once designed. Her once crisp-looking slacks now hung like wrinkled gunnysack and her auburn hair had lost its curl and clung in a matted tangle close to her head. Jane knew she undoubtedly looked just as unkempt.

"Excuse me," Jane said when it seemed the two of them would go on talking forever. "I wonder if we could go back to the house. I'd like to get out of these wet clothes."

Katrin appeared startled, as if she'd forgotten Jane was there. "Sure," she said finally. "You'd better get some of Aunt Lizzie's breakfast, too, before it's all gone. I'm afraid you're already too late for the muffins."

"I'm sure we can make do," Jane said as they walked toward the house.

"I just can't imagine how y'all got yourselves locked inside the Bean Farm." Katrin watched the ground as she spoke, so she could maneuver around the headstones.

"The what?" Jane and Hillary asked together.

"Bean Farm. Winston gave the place that name. You know, where all the Beans are planted?"

"Oh. Yeah, I see," Jane said.

"Beans? Planted here?" Hillary said. She looked around as if she was searching for bean stalks.

"Anyway," Katrin said, ignoring Hillary, "that gate hasn't been locked in years. We leave it open because, as I said, we take turns caring for the place. I had a terrible time finding the key."

"Strange," Jane said. "But then there seemed to me to be a lot of strange things about the funeral."

"Really? What?" Katrin wore a look of surprise.

Jane exchanged a quick glance with Hillary before she spoke, and, judging by Hillary's expression, she was just as eager for some answers as Jane was. "Well, for one thing," Jane said, "that minister."

"What about him?" Katrin had gone back to navigating through the headstones.

"Did he—well—did he look familiar to you?" Jane was being cautious. She wasn't sure just how to start this fishing expedition.

"Familiar?" Katrin seemed genuinely puzzled. "No, I'd never seen him before. I don't get up to Birmingham much."

Jane tried again. "He left right after the service, didn't he?"

"I believe so."

"Did he have any reason to come back? After dark, I mean?"

"Why no, why would he?" The puzzled frown on Katrin's face deepened.

"I thought maybe he came back to, well, maybe pick up someone," Jane said, still probing.

"There's no earthly reason for him to pick up anyone." Katrin had begun to look at Jane with a hint of either concern or impatience for her obtuseness.

"Earthly reason? How about unearthly?" Hillary's voice was edgy again. "Those noises last night. Did you hear them?"

"Noises?" Katrin said. "No, I didn't hear a thing. Except the storm. And the wind in the trees. I think maybe this place is starting to get to you. I know it gets to me sometimes."

"Then why don't you leave?" Jane asked.

Katrin looked up at her with a startled expression, as if she'd never considered that idea. "Leave? How could I? I'm a Bean."

"But there must have been other Beans who have left," Jane said. They were nearing the house now, close to the spot where the car had stopped the night before.

"Of course there have been Beans and relatives of the Beans who have left, but there's always a price to pay. Winston left once. Ask him. Now, because of him, we all have to stay," Katrin said.

Jane frowned, puzzled. "I don't understand."

"No, you wouldn't understand." Katrin opened the front door, then turned around to look at Jane and Hillary before she entered. "But you should both leave as soon as you can, even if I can't."

12

Jane had showered and changed into the clothes Lotus had provided for her the first evening they were there. She had washed her hair and was pulling it back into a butterscotch ponytail when Hillary walked into her room. The ponytail was a style she'd adopted when she was in law school because it was quick and easy. Jim Ed had hated it. Said it made her look like a teenager. Then he married Miss Alabama, who was still using Clearasil, although she filled out her training bra quite nicely.

Hillary had washed her hair, but it hung like damp wallpaper, plastered close to her head. Since neither of them expected to be here this long, Hillary hadn't brought her hair dryer or her full cache of makeup. She wore only the lipstick, mascara, and powder from a compact she carried in her purse. The lipstick didn't match the green dress, and her mascara, usually applied with such great care, was smudged. Obviously their sojourn at the Beans' was getting to her.

"Do you think I look all right?" Hillary was patting her hair, smoothing her skirt, and wearing a worried frown.

"You look—fine." Jane nodded her head and creased her brow with her own worried frown. Now wasn't the time to destroy Hillary's confidence. They had problems enough.

"You are lyin' to me, Jane." Hillary walked to the mirror to look at her image. "I'm not sure this color is right for me, and my hair . . . Oh Lord, hon, just look at me! I look awful." She started to cry.

"You don't look awful," Jane lied. She went to her and put her arms around her, patting her back as she tried to comfort her. She pulled a tissue from a box on the nightstand and dabbed it at Hillary's eyes, trying to soak up the mascara that was now streaming down her face like a murky river. "Come on," she coaxed, "let's go see what's left for breakfast." She took Hillary's hand and led her downstairs.

In the dining room, Lotus still sat at the table, munching on a piece of bacon while she stared absently into space. Muddy pools of weariness stagnated under her eyes.

"Good mornin', Lotus." Hillary's drawl lacked some of its usual vitality. It was hard to tell whether it was because she still suspected Lotus of murder or because she was upset about her looks.

Lotus glanced at the two of them and nodded almost imperceptibly.

"Are you all right, Lotus?" Jane asked. It was as good a way as any to try once again to drag some information from her.

Lotus's answer was a sigh as she reached for another serving of bacon.

Jane tried again. "Is something wrong?" As she spoke, she heard the telephone ring in another part of the house. Her first thought was that it was Jim Ed calling to tell her something was wrong with Sarah, but she forced the thought from her mind. She had to get over her anxiety about her daughter.

Lotus looked at her, and this time there were tears in her eyes. "It's Hieronymus. She's disappeared." Hope shone for a brief moment on her face. "You haven't seen her have you?"

"Seen her?" Hillary seemed agitated. "We spent the night with her."

Lotus put down her bacon. "You did? She was in your room? Is she still there?"

"Not in my room. In the graveyard."

"What?"

"Oh my Lord, yes," Hillary said with a wave of her now unmanicured hand. "It was just the most awful thing."

"But why?"

"Why? Because somebody locked the gate, and we got trapped in there. I don't suppose you know anything about that, do you?" Hillary's usual Southern charm had been replaced with irritability.

"Who was trapped? I don't know anything about anybody being trapped. But you said Hieronymus was in there with you?"

"Yes, until this mornin', when Katrin came and opened the door. Hieronymus ran out of there like her tail was on fire."

Lotus picked up the remaining bacon from the platter and pushed away from the table, standing as if she was about to leave.

Jane suddenly remembered the figure they'd seen from the window of the shed, draped with a shawl and walking among the headstones. Katrin had dismissed the sighting as the ghost of America Elizabeth. "Lotus," Jane said, "were you by chance looking for Hieronymus in the cemetery last night?"

"I just don't see how she could have gotten out with the doors closed." Lotus said, as if she hadn't heard Jane. "I looked all over this house, and then I didn't get any sleep because I was so worried about her."

"But did you go out to the—" Before Jane could finish her sentence, Lizzie entered the room with an announcement.

"Sheriff Harkelrode just called."

"Oh God!" Jane said. A sheriff is always the one calling to give the bad news, she thought. "Was there a message? It wasn't about my little girl, was it?" she managed to ask, in spite of the fact that her throat seemed to be closing with anxiety.

"There was a message." Lizzie spoke with her usual grimness.

"And . . . ?"

"Said to tell you the bridge will be fixed tomorrow. Seems somebody back there in Prosper has some political connections."

"Billy!" Hillary was beaming. "Beau must have called Billy! That man is absolutely remarkable."

"Tomorrow? Tuesday?" Jane was remembering that Sarah was due to come home Tuesday. She wouldn't have to call Jim Ed after all. She had yet to meet Billy Scarborough in person, but when she did, she was going to give him a big hug.

"Well, that means we have to get busy and start to work for the party tonight." The good news made Hillary sound like her old self again and apparently she'd forgot her suspicion of Lotus.

"Oh yes, the wake," Lotus said, brightening a little.

"Wake. Yes, that's what I meant." Hillary wrinkled her brow. "But it's still a party, isn't it? Sort of like a deathday party?"

"It is! Yes, that's exactly what it is. A deathday party." Lotus's expression changed again. Her troubled frown had returned. But I really ought to find Hieronymus first."

Jane saw disappointment make Hillary's bright expression disintegrate like ashes in the wind. "Tell you what," Jane said. "I'll look for Hieronymus. You help Hillary with the food for tonight." It was best to keep Hillary's spirits up until they could drive across that bridge and home again, she thought, and it would give her time to do some more sniffing around.

Lotus agreed enthusiastically. "I've looked in this house from top to bottom. But if you saw her outdoors . . ."

"Don't worry, Lotus, I'll find her." Jane wasn't at all sure she could, but she would have promised anything for an excuse to snoop around.

The rain of the evening before had left the air sticky with humidity, but Jane walked across the grounds looking for some sign of Cassandra, in spite of the discomfort. She wasn't sure what she was looking for, or even if Cassandra was still around, but with the bridge out, she couldn't be too far away. Twenty minutes later, her borrowed dress was circled with rings of perspiration, and her hair felt as wet as it had when she'd come out of the shower, but she still had found neither Hieronymus nor any sign of Cassandra.

Jane had just come around to the front of the house when she heard the sound of a car approaching from the back road. She felt her body tense. This car, of course, could be any one of the neighbors who lived on this side of the bridge. Still, she couldn't forget the car she'd seen last night and the mysterious figure in white who might have got into the car before it drove away.

The auto, an older luxury model, slightly faded from the sun, stopped in front of the Bean house. But instead of some mysterious figure getting out, it was only Winston. His face simmered with anger, and he closed the car door with a violent push. Then, looking up, he saw Jane, and the anger disappeared like a magician's trick under the white handkerchief of a smile.

"Jane! Dear! What a surprise to see you. You're surely not out to enjoy the day. Such dreadful weather."

Jane wiped some of the sweat off her forehead with her arm. "No, just looking for Hieronymus."

"That pesky beast? Lotus's familiar, I call it. We'd all be better off if she disappeared forever." Winston's eyes darted about as if he was searching for the cat, in spite of his words.

"I'm sure Lotus doesn't feel that way," Jane said.

"What?" Winston seemed distracted. "Oh, no, I suppose not."

"You haven't see her anywhere, have you?" Jane asked.

"I've been spared that aggravation at least."

Jane looked at him, curious. "Had a bad morning, I take it."

"A what? Oh, no, no, of course not." Winston's manufactured smile slipped back into place. "Had a nice visit with Cousin Chester, actually."

"You mean Chester Collins?"

"Yes, yes, the family's man of the cloth." Winston was moving toward the front door of the house. "I told him you were here. He sends his regards," he said over his shoulder just as he disappeared into the house.

"Oh, yeah, I'm sure he did," Jane said aloud to herself as she moved away, looking for Hieronymus again. Chester Collins, she felt sure, had little regard for her. It was in his role as an alderman for the city of Prosper that she'd made him angry once when she'd confronted him with the free-wheeling way he spent taxpayers' money on luxury items for himself and his mistress. She had no idea how he kept all his shenanigans away from the eyes and ears of his flock.

Jane moved out farther into the front garden of the house. As she walked past Winston's car, she gave a cursory glance through one of the windows. What she saw made her stop and look again. There was something on the floor in the back. Something white and gauzy.

After a quick glance around her to make sure no one was watching, Jane tried the door in the back. It wasn't locked. She opened the door and quickly pulled the white fabric out of the car and held it up for a better look. It was a woman's long white gown made with a generously full skirt, and it was damp, as if whoever last wore it had been caught in the rain.

Was this the car she and Hillary had seen stop in front of the house last night? Had Winston been driving it? Was Cassandra the woman in white who had gotten inside?

There were too many unanswered questions, and whatever the answers turned out to be, they would only serve to point out just how creepy this place was, Jane thought.

Suddenly she heard a noise—a faint sound—but it startled her, and she threw the soggy white gown back into the car and closed the door. Drying her hands on the back of her dress, she looked all around her. The sound seemed to have come from her left, the direction of the family plot. She glanced at it, half expecting to see ethereal spirits rising from the gravestones. All she saw was Katrin walking across the expanse of lawn between the graveyard and the house. Apparently, the noise she had heard was Katrin closing the gate after she had finished her gardening.

Jane turned around with a sigh of relief just in time to see eyes looking at her from inside the car.

She stifled a scream with a hand to her mouth, then relaxed when she saw that the eyes belonged Hieronymus. She was trapped inside the car, and those eyes shone with anger because of her plight. She wore a puffy black grosgrain bow around her neck that did nothing to soften her expression. There had been no bow around her neck when she spent the night in the cemetery's tool shed. Jane opened the door to the front seat and Hieronymus jumped out, sharing her feelings with the world with a screeching protest.

Jane ran after Hieronymus and, stooping quickly, caught the cat up in her arms just as she reached the house. Still holding the cat, Jane turned her attention to Katrin as she drew closer.

"What's that you've got there?" Katrin asked

"Hieronymus," Jane said. "She was trapped in the car. Winston must have taken her with him when he went to see Chester, only I don't think he knew she was in the car."

"Winston went to see Chester? Why?" Katrin looked surprised.

Jane shrugged. "Just a friendly visit, I guess. Couple of relatives who haven't seen each other in a while."

"Winston and Chester don't even know each other."

"Oh, I see," Jane said, although she didn't see at all.

"Hieronymus?" Katrin said as she reached out to touch the cat. "That's funny," she said.

"What's funny?"

"That ribbon. Lotus hates those things. The only person who ever put them on Hieronymus was Cassandra. She and Lotus were always fighting over that cat."

"But Cassandra is dead. How could she put the ribbon on her?" Jane was once again testing.

"Yes." Katrin wore a troubled expression, as if even a Bean would find that strange.

"So then, who do you think put this on her?" Jane asked, fingering the ribbon.

Katrin shook her head. "Oh dear," she said, half under her breath. "I hope we're not going to have another ghost. There's only so much of this a person can take, you know." She moved past Jane and into the house, still shaking her head.

When Jane walked into the library with Hieronymus in her arms, Lotus glanced up anxiously from her work with Hillary. Rather than the elated expression Jane expected because Hieronymus had been found, Lotus turned pallid, and a look of alarm punctuated her eyes.

"I found her in Winston's car," Jane said, puzzled at Lotus's reaction. "She must have gotten trapped in there somehow when he went to see your Cousin Chester."

Lotus didn't answer. She snatched the cat from Jane's arms and untied the black ribbon, wadded it, and threw it into the open mouth of the fireplace with the other debris that had collected there.

"Sorry about the ribbon," Jane said, testing her. "Katrin said it's usually Cassandra who puts them on her. Said you hate them."

"Katrin's wrong." Lotus's voice was edged with emotion. Was it anger or fear? "It wasn't Cassandra. I put the ribbon on her."

"When, Lotus?" Jane moved slightly closer to Lotus, a technique she'd observed Jim Ed using in the courtroom when he wanted to be particularly intimidating. "She didn't have the ribbon on when she was in the cemetery with us last night, and you said you hadn't seen her this morning."

There was no mistaking the fear in Lotus's eyes this time. "Of course I saw her. It was—it was only later that she disappeared."

The nervous fluttering of her hands and the fact that her frightened eyes failed to meet Jane's gave her away. She was lying. But why? "Lotus," Jane began, ready to try to force the truth from her. But before she could say more, Hillary called from a table at the other end of the library where a mound of flowers lay in front of her.

"Jane, dear, could you lend me a hand?" Hillary was busy arranging the flowers in vases. "We're running out of time. The wake starts at seven tonight. Lotus has already called everyone.''

Lotus had taken the distraction as an opportunity to move quickly away from Jane and out of the library.

''All right, what do you want me to do?'' Jane asked with a sigh. ''Looks like you've got the flower arrangements well in hand. Shall I help Lizzie with the cooking?''

''Oh Lord no!'' Hillary's eyes shone with alarm. ''Don't you dare go near that kitchen, Jane Ferguson.'' She handed Jane a circular frame, which she had fashioned out of grapevine. ''We're going to make wreaths out of this foxglove and baby's breath. See, all you do is weave it like this,'' she said, demonstrating to Jane how to intertwine the flowers on the frame. The wreath was lovely when she finished. ''Now, if you think you've got the hang of this, Jane, I'm going to help Lizzie with the menu.''

''How hard can it be?'' Jane picked up one of the frames in one hand and a long stem of foxglove in the other.

Within a few minutes, she found out exactly how hard it could be. She'd broken at least a dozen of the long stems. It took her half an hour to finish a single wreath, and it looked nothing at all like the one Hillary had created. Flowers and stems stuck out at crazy angles as if they had somehow been mangled by the grapevine rather than entwined around it.

''You've never done this before?'' Hillary asked when she came back to the library to inspect Jane's work. ''You told me you were experienced with cooking and crafts when I hired you last September,'' she said before Jane could answer.

''I guess I've just been too busy going to law school, and I'm out of practice.''

Hillary shook her head. ''If you weren't so clever at accounting and at dealing with all the people I have to work with, I'd fire you.''

''As I recall, you *did* fire me, and I don't remember being reinstated.''

''Don't be tiresome, Jane,'' Hillary said over her shoulder as she started to leave. ''I have a ham to see to.''

Jane sighed and looked at her work. Hillary was right. It did leave something to be desired.

"Is something wrong? Katrin asked as she entered the library. She glanced at the mess Jane had made, then went to a bookshelf. "Looks like the *Digitalis purpurea* got the best of you." She ran a finger along the books' spines, searching.

"I'm afraid I'm not very good at making decorative wreaths," Jane said.

Katrin pulled a book from the shelf and tucked it under her arm. Jane could read at least one word in the title: *Botany*. Katrin glanced at Jane with her usual serious expression. "Don't concern yourself. There are more important uses for those plants," she said as she left the room.

Jane sighed again, then got up to go to her room, thinking that perhaps the best thing she could do was stay out of the way while preparations for the party continued. She had just reached the door to her room when she noticed the door to the adjoining room—Cassandra's room—was slightly ajar. She had chided Hillary for being nosy and going in there, but now she was tempted to do the same thing. She had no idea what she could expect to find, but she was becoming even more determined to get to the bottom of the strange goings-on.

With a quick glance around her to make sure no one was in the hall, she stepped hurriedly next door and carefully pushed the door open. An assortment of women's clothes was strewn on the bed that had now replaced the casket. A pair of sandals and one odd sneaker lay carelessly on the floor. And on top of the bureau was a spool of black grosgrain ribbon with a pair of scissors next to it.

13

"A spool of black ribbon on Cassandra's bureau? So what?" Hillary was in Jane's room, trying, with little success, to arrange her flattened hair.

"Don't you see what that means, Hillary? It means someone was in there cutting that ribbon to tie around Hieronymus's neck." Jane was sitting on the bed, waiting for Hillary to finish dressing so they could go downstairs to the wake.

"So?" Hillary leaned closer to the mirror to inspect her makeup-free skin and frowned in disapproval.

"It had to be Cassandra."

Hillary turned away from the mirror wearing a startled expression. "What are you getting at, Jane?"

"Well, think about it, Hillary. Katrin said Cassandra was the only one who ever tied ribbons around Hieronymus."

"Anyone could have decided to tie a ribbon around that cat's neck." Hillary put her hand to her forehead and closed her eyes. "I'm getting a headache, Jane. I'm not used to analyzing things like this. You're the one who's good at that kind of thing." She opened her eyes and looked at Jane with a serious expression. "Don't do this to me."

Jane stood and paced the floor. "You're right. Of course

it could have been Winston or Julia who tied that ribbon.''

"Of course. Now you sound like the old Jane." Hillary went back to fussing with her hair.

"Still . . ."

"Still what?" Hillary raised a suspicious eyebrow and looked at Jane's image behind her in the mirror.

"I don't know. It's just that . . . Well, that figure we saw getting into Winston's car, and then the wet shroud in the backseat—it all seems so . . ."

Hillary turned suddenly away from the mirror. "Shroud? What shroud?"

Jane glanced at Hillary. "I didn't tell you, did I? You were so busy planning the party . . ."

"Didn't tell me what?"

"When I opened the back door of Winston's car to let Hieronymus out, that's when I saw it.

"Saw what?"

"The shroud. Lying on the floor in the back of the car. A white shroud. And it was wet."

Hillary frowned. "A shroud? A wet shroud? What does that mean? That there's a naked ghost walking around somewhere?"

Jane sat down heavily on the bed, feeling frustrated, maybe even a little defeated. "I'm not sure what it means, except that whoever was wearing it—Cassandra I assume— must have been in Winston's car at some point. Maybe it means it was Winston's car that pulled up in front of the house and Cassandra got in his car."

"And Winston was driving it?"

"That seems logical."

Hillary shook her head. "Jane, honey, haven't you said it yourself over and over again that none of this makes sense?"

"You're right, Hill." Jane sighed and stood up, extending a hand toward Hillary. "Come on. Let's go down to that party."

Hillary gave her a surprised look. "Are you actually showing a little enthusiasm for one of my parties? You've never done that before."

Jane shrugged. "I'm just thinking about what you said about Chester Collins. Remember? You said he might give us some insight into things. Well, I thought I would find out if you're right."

"What would you do without me?" Hillary said with a confident smile.

As soon as they got downstairs and into the parlor, Hillary began to mingle, moving around with her droopy hairdo, her broken nails, and her inappropriate green dress, making sure everyone had enough punch and hors d'oeuvres.

Jane was a little taken aback at the mood of the crowd. It was a strange wake. Not only was there no corpse, since bringing Bruce's body back by helicopter was expensive and impractical, but the guests didn't seem properly subdued; in fact, they seemed to be having a good time. Even Lizzie looked mildly pleasant. Of course, all along, the wake had been nothing more than a thinly veiled excuse for a party. Lotus, however, who had been the most enthusiastic about the prospects of a party, now appeared almost distraught as she sat alone in the corner of the parlor twisting the end of her tunic while Hieronymus coiled at her feet.

The guests, actually, were few in number, since only those on one side of the bridge could come. There were no more than twenty people present. Chester Collins was among them. He sat on an old-fashioned sofa, deep in conversation with Winston, a plate of hors d'oeuvres balanced on one knee and a glass of punch in his hand. Katrin had said they didn't even know each other, which, in itself was odd, since everyone else knew every other relative. But, as she had told herself before, odd was normal for the Beans. As soon as Chester saw Jane, he gave her an artificial smile, then excused himself from Winston and stood to make his way across the room to her side.

"Miz Ferguson! You can't imagine how surprised I was to learn that you and that—that partner of yours were here. I heard y'all got stuck out here when the bridge washed out. But don't you worry your pretty little heads. I plan to make some phone calls tomorrow and use my connections to get that bridge fixed.''

"You do that, Chester."

Chester took out a handkerchief and wiped his forehead. "Lord, how long must we endure? A man like me doesn't belong in the sticks like this. What I mean is, I have the Lord's work to . . ."

Chester didn't finish his sentence as his eyes fell upon a particularly shapely young woman standing near the punch bowl wearing a low-cut dress and plenty of makeup.

"Well, God works in mysterious ways, as they say," Jane said, watching him ogle.

"My oh my! I mean, yes. Yes, he does, doesn't he?" Chester said, moving his eyes quickly back to Jane.

"I take it you're feeling better?" Jane asked.

Chester was still distracted, still having a difficult time keeping his eyes off the young woman. "Feeling who? I mean what?"

"Better. Feeling better."

"Oh yes, yes. Much better, thank you. Sorry I couldn't be here for Cousin Cassandra's funeral, but we did the breast—uh, best we could, under the circumstances. We sent a substitute." Chester had a habit of using the imperial we, as if he, himself, might be the king of heaven, Jane thought.

"Oh yes, the Reverend Johnston. How did you come to know him?"

Chester looked surprised. "Know him? Why, I never met him before yesterday when Winston introduced him to me."

"Winston introduced you?"

"Yes. Must have known Winston before he entered the ministry. Winston doesn't have much to do with the Lord's work, I'm afraid. Prefers the den of iniquity."

"Den of iniquity?" Jane asked.

"Oh yes. Oh yes. He was just telling me about his past." Chester leaned his portly frame closer to Jane. "He used to be a bartender in Birmingham," he said in a hushed tone. "Birmingham is full of sin! Why, he even smoked dope once and took guitar lessons."

"No!"

Chester nodded. "Besides that, he got involved with the Birmingham Community Theater."

"Bless my soul!"

Chester nodded and put on a smug, satisfied expression. "No telling what else he was up to while he was up there in Birmingham. Just got back, you know. Birmingham is no place for a Bean. Tends to attract people of loose morals."

"Oh?"

"It's not that I'm against good clean fun, Miz Ferguson." Chester gave her a concerned frown.

"I'm sure you're not."

"Oh no. The Lord wants us to enjoy ourselves. He wants us to go to the picture show and to theater and to concerts, but he doesn't approve of the loose morals of the people in those industries."

"He's told you this, I suppose."

"I speak with the Lord on a daily basis, Miz Ferguson."

"And he speaks back."

"Of course." Chester had now assumed his most pious expression. "If we just open our hearts, we will hear. It is my greatest burden that I could not convince Cassandra before she departed this earth to meet our Lord face-to-face."

"Cassandra? I've been wanting to talk to you about her. Do you know any reason why—"

"Why she wouldn't change her ways? Lord knows, I don't. Why, I've been on my knees more than once praying for her immortal soul. But as is his way, the devil was right on her tail and lured her into a trap: the satanic powers of the zodiac." Chester's voice had taken on a singsong preacher's cadence. This time, he quickly put on a saddened expression, like an actor donning a mask. "She was called to the great accounting before I could make her see the error of her ways. The Lord giveth and the Lord taketh away, and if we are not ready when the trumpet sounds for our soul, then we will surely perish in the pits of—"

"Hell, Cousin Chester." Winston emerged, a punch cup in hand and a teasing smile on his lips.

"What?" Chester looked at him, flustered.

"Hell," Winston said again. "Isn't that where we will perish if we don't mend our ways?" He gave Jane a conspiratorial wink. "Lord, how long must we suffer?"

"How long, indeed," Chester said. He was obviously annoyed with Winston.

"I suppose he's been telling you about the evils of this world, and Birmingham in particular," Winston said, glancing at Jane again.

"On the contrary," Chester said, drawing himself up in a self-righteous way. "There's nothing inherently wrong with the world, which the Lord has made with his own hands. It is unfortunate, though, that it has become infected with those of loose morals. And consorting with them endangers your soul."

"Well, you can rest easy about my soul," Winston said. "I've left that life behind."

Chester's eyes widened. "Praise the Lord. Brother Johnston must have had some influence."

"Oh yes," Winston said. Jane couldn't tell whether Winston's response was in earnest or if he was still mocking Chester.

Chester beamed. "The Lord hears those who pray without ceasing." He cleared his throat. "Now, if you'll excuse me, I believe I will sample some more of the tidbits you've provided before I say a few words about dear Cousin Bruce and America Elizabeth, as Lotus has asked me to do."

"Of course," Winston said. Jane watched, frustrated, as Chester moved to·the end of the refreshment table where the voluptuous young woman was standing. She was obviously the tidbit he had in mind. The young woman was talking with a grieving Julia, who had finally come downstairs. Chester picked up Julia's hand and held it between both of his, speaking to her in quiet tones, but his eyes kept moving to the younger woman's bosom.

"So you've just returned from Birmingham?" Jane said, turning her attention back to Winston.

"And none too soon."

"Oh?"

Winston laughed. "Not because it's a den of iniquity. Cousin Chester sees the devil everywhere, doesn't he?"

Jane glanced at Chester, who now had the young woman by the arm and was leading her away, talking all the while. Julia had collapsed in a chair next to the one Lotus had been sitting in, but Lotus was now nowhere in sight.

"Well, not quite everywhere," she said. She turned back to Winston. "How is it that you never met Cousin Chester before?"

Winston raised an eyebrow. "It's a large family. Can't get around to everyone."

"But everyone else seems to know—"

"Now, now, Miz Ferguson, don't try to figure out the Bean family. We all have our eccentricities, you know."

Jane tried another tactic. "Chester said Reverend Johnston is a friend of yours."

"Acquaintance, actually. Met him in Birmingham."

"I see. Tell me, Winston, don't you think he bears a striking resemblance to the telephone repairman who was here earlier?"

Winston laughed. "That's an old joke—accusing us Southerners of inbreeding and saying we all look alike." He glanced over her shoulder. "Oh, excuse me, I believe he just came in," Winston said. Jane followed his gaze to the wide doorway leading to the entry hall. Reverend Johnston was, indeed, just entering. Winston moved away to greet him, and Jane would have joined them if Hillary hadn't tapped her on the shoulder at just that moment and told her she was needed in the kitchen. As she left the parlor, she noticed that Lotus still had not returned.

In a little while, Winston announced that Chester would speak, and the group grew quiet. Hillary and Jane came back to the parlor from the kitchen. Chester droned on in his TV-evangelist style about Bruce's life, his soul, his place in heaven, and the risk of hellfire and damnation everyone faced if they didn't subscribe to Chester's particular brand of religion. He was playing his part, and every-

one listened politely. When he finished, he read an equally
long and boring piece someone had handed him about
America Elizabeth: where she was born, when she had died,
how her spirit still watched over the family.

Lotus still had not returned when the service ended. Jane
asked Hillary and Katrin and Winston each if they'd seen
her, but no one had.

Even Julia, who apparently had been the last to speak to
her, shook her head. "She excused herself. Said she had a
headache. Maybe she went to her room," Julia said.

"Lotus? No, I haven't seen her," Chester said when Jane
asked him about her. "There's no telling where she is.
Strange girl. A bit touched in the head. The Bean side of
the family, all of them, they've always been the odd ones."
He leaned toward Jane and whispered, "And it was that
America Elizabeth that started it all." Jane could smell liq
uor on his breath, as if he'd had more than his share of
Hillary's very potent punch.

"What do you mean?" Jane asked.

"Well, see, she was the one built this house, and she was
the one bought the land way back there before the War
Between the States. And she wrote it in her will that the
land was going to be passed down through the family, but
it had to be the daughter of a daughter that got the land.
No boys could get it, see, and she said she would always
be around after death to see that the land was taken care
of. Ever'body says she killed that woman who was trying
to get the land away from her. Only the woman was already
dead. You heard that story?"

"I've heard it," Jane said.

Chester shook his head. "Like I said, odd bunch. I'm
only slightly related to them, you know. Third cousin twice
removed. They've got problems. Big problems, if you
know what I mean."

"Problems?"

Chester nodded. The liquor, obviously, had loosened his
tongue. "Financial problems," he whispered. "I suppose
you know about that."

"No!" Jane said, pretending to be shocked, but she was

remembering the dilapidated condition of the house.

"Well, all this belongs to Aunt Lizzie now, but she never had a daughter. Never married, as a matter of fact, so now there's a big family feud. Looks to me like they're going to feud their way into bankruptcy and lose the land."

"That's too bad," Jane said. But that may explain a few things, she thought.

"Vengeance is mine, sayeth the Lord. It's retribution for their sins, I say. All that messing with the zodiac, and no telling what all."

"Really?" Jane said.

"Poor Aunt Lizzie. She just doesn't have the financial smarts to keep it. I just pray that Winston chap will look after her best interests."

"Winston?"

Chester nodded again. "Just said he's about to come into some money."

"Oh, really? He told you that, did he?"

"Didn't tell me. I overheard him telling that young woman. Said he was going to buy this place for himself. I just hope he lets Aunt Lizzie and Aunt Julia stay here if he does, poor souls."

"He's a Bean, isn't he?" Jane said. "Doesn't that count for something? When it comes to taking care of their own, I mean."

"Oh he's a Bean, all right. Connected through Lizzie's grandfather's brother, I think. Distant relative. But who knows if he'll take care of 'em or not. If you want to know what I think, I think he was just bragging about that money to get that young woman's attention. I'll say he's broke as any of 'em, and this place is going for taxes!"

Hillary walked by, carrying a tray of food, and Chester helped himself to several servings. "Delicious," he said, which made Hillary beam with pleasure.

"Have you tried the punch?" she asked. "Come, let me get you some. She led him away before Jane was finished questioning him, but she felt grateful that she had learned at least as much as she had.

All the guests began to leave soon after that, but Jane

stayed to help Hillary with the cleaning, and it was another hour before they went upstairs to their rooms.

"It went well, didn't it?" Hillary said as they made their way up. "The ham was wonderful, and you should have seen Lizzie when I showed her how to shave it thin. Absolutely astounded! Her expression actually changed, which is something for her, don't you think? Oh, and the foxglove held up much better than I expected. The wreaths were the perfect touch! Did you notice I used that black ribbon you found? I know it's Cassandra's, but how could she mind if she's, you know, passed on? Do you think Lotus was pleased? What happened to her? Odd that she disappeared, don't you think?"

Hillary went on, nonstop, until they reached Jane's door. "Good night, Hillary," Jane said. Kitchen duty and catering always exhausted her, and she would have been too tired to answer Hillary's endless questions, even if she'd given her a chance. She would share all the information she'd gathered from the guests later.

"Ta-ta," Hillary said, still exuberant, as Jane opened the door to her room.

As soon as Jane stepped into her room, she knew someone had been there. It was not that the room had been disturbed, it was a simply a sense of a presence having been there or perhaps still being there. She took a few cautious steps farther into the room, her eyes searching, her mind alert.

She heard a scream from down the hall. It sounded like Hillary, and she felt a rush of adrenaline. At the same moment, she saw the sheet of paper on her bed. Her first instinct was to rush to Hillary. She had just reached the door again when Hillary pushed her way inside. The blood had drained from her face, and her eyes were wide.

"Oh my Lord, Jane, it was awful. Did you hear it?" She put a hand to her forehead. "How much more of this can I take! You've got to get me out of here! Do you hear? I want to go now!"

"Calm down, Hillary," Jane said in the most soothing voice she could manage. "Come on, sit here on the bed.

Tell me what happened." She picked up the sheet of paper as she helped Hillary sit down.

"Calm down? How can I calm down? This house is haunted! There are spirits. Evil spirits. I heard them!"

"What are you talking about, Hillary?"

"Didn't you hear it?" Hillary was still wide-eyed and pale. "A thumping and a kind of moaning."

"I didn't hear a thing. Except your scream."

"But you must have. It was . . . What's that you've got in your hand?"

"This was on my bed when I came in," Jane said. "I didn't get a chance to look at it because you came . . . Oh my God, this is a note from Lotus!"

Hillary frowned, puzzled. "Lotus? Why would she leave a note?"

"Listen to this." Jane read the note. " 'You have been kind and generous, and because of that I must warn you to leave the house as soon as possible. Your lives are in danger. Don't wait for the bridge to be repaired. I hope you understand that I have gone to join Cassandra.' "

Jane showed Hillary the paper. "Look, it's signed with a drawing of a lotus flower."

Hillary had grown even more pale. "My Lord, Jane. She's gone to join Cassandra? Does that means she has taken her own life?"

Jane shook her head. "I don't know."

Hillary took the paper from her. "And what was that about our lives being in danger?" She scanned the note quickly, then closed her eyes and fell back on the bed. "Oh my God, we're going to die!"

Jane retrieved the paper from where Hillary had dropped it beside her on the bed. "Not without a fight, we're not."

Hillary opened her eyes suddenly. "There it is again!" she said. "Did you hear that?"

"Hear what? I don't hear anything."

"There! That sound. A thumping. Only it's louder in my room. I heard it when I first went in, and there was moaning and . . . Oh my Lord, the most unearthly sound you can imagine."

Jane held a hand up as a signal for Hillary to be quiet. "Shhh. Yes, I think I heard something," she whispered."

"I told you, it's spirits. Evil spirits," Hillary whispered in reply.

"No, it's someone in that passageway that leads down to the basement," Jane said. She grabbed her small flashlight from the bedside table and started for the door.

"Where are you going?" Hillary called after her.

"I'm going to open up that secret doorway in your room and see what's down there." Jane was already on her way up the hallway to Hillary's room."

"Jane, are you crazy?" Hillary was now following closely behind.

Jane didn't answer, and within seconds she was in Hillary's room, pushing back the bureau and propping the doorway open with a chair. She stepped into the darkened passage with the tiny beam of light shining on the step in front of her.

"Jane! Come back here!" Hillary called in a hoarse whisper. It was only a few seconds more before Jane sensed Hillary making her way down the stairs, then sticking close behind her.

When they reached the first landing, Jane was surprised to see a sliver of light seeping from under the wall at the landing ahead of her. Slowly and carefully, she continued her way down the creaky staircase.

"What's that?" Hillary whispered, pointing to the light.

"I don't know," Jane said. "Must be light coming from one of the rooms on this floor."

"Oh, of course." Hillary sounded relieved for a moment, then her voice was tense again as she whispered, "The murderer's room maybe?"

"I don't think so," Jane said. "We're on the same level as the dining room and the living areas. Maybe a closet or something. We've got other things to worry about now, though," she said, giving her flashlight a shake. The beam was growing noticeably dimmer, and then it went out.

Hillary sucked in her breath, frightened. Jane shook the flashlight again, trying in vain to make it work. They were

now in almost total darkness. There was only the tiny slice
of light coming from underneath the wall at the landing.
Jane went to the wall and felt along it with her fingertips
and tapped on it with the useless flashlight.

"What are you doing?" Hillary asked.

"Looking for an opening. If I can find one, we'll have
some light." Suddenly, the light that had been seeping from
under the wall went out as well, and the darkness closed
around them in a cold embrace.

"What are we going to do?" Hillary whispered, sounding more frightened than ever.

"Let's go on downstairs," Jane said. "I still want to see
if there's someone in that basement."

"That's just what I'm afraid of!" Hillary took Jane's
arm and tried to pull her back, but Jane shrugged her off
and started down the stairs.

They were at the last landing when they heard a screech
coming from somewhere in the passage behind them. Hillary screamed and grabbed at Jane, causing her to lose her
balance. Jane found herself falling down the last of the
steps, and when she landed, she fell upon what she knew
was a dead body.

14

Within seconds, Hillary had landed on top of Jane. They both scrambled to their feet, and in the process, Hillary stumbled over the body. She screamed.

"Shhh!" Jane cautioned.

Hillary grabbed her and screamed again.

"Hillary! Quiet!"

"Quiet? Why? It's not going to hear us. It's dead!" Hillary's voice was squeaky with fright.

"But someone else might."

"Who?"

Jane was groping in the dark, trying to find her way around the body. "I don't know. Maybe whoever killed this poor soul. Maybe the murderer will hear us."

"He's here?" Hillary's voice squeaked a decibel higher.

"I don't know," Jane whispered. She was now feeling along the shelves of the cellar, looking for the lantern she had seen there earlier. Finally she found it, and she felt along the shelf again until she felt the matches under her fingertips.

"Jane? Jane, where are you? What are you doing?"

Jane answered by striking a match. In the light of the weak flame she saw Hillary put her hand over her mouth and stifle another scream. Jane tried to light the lantern, but the match went out before she could touch it to the wick. She shook the lantern and could tell it was out of fuel.

"Damn," she said under her breath and reached for another match. This time when it lit, she held it in the direction of the body lying on the floor, and saw immediately what had given Hillary a second shock. The body was that of Reverend Johnston. His eyes were open and fixed, and he wore an expression of great surprise. Beside him was a pool of vomit. They had just missed falling in it.

When the match went out, Jane reached for another one, struck it on the wooden shelf, and once again held it close to the body. This time she looked for the telltale marks in the cellar's dirt floor that she'd seen before when she and Hillary had found Bruce's body just a few feet away. The floor showed no sign of marks this time, but before the match burned out, Jane saw that the backs of Reverend Johnston's boots were encrusted with mud.

"Was that mud?" Hillary asked, bending to examine the boots just before the flame burned out.

"Yes."

"Then he was dragged, too?"

"I think so."

"Who dragged him here? And why?" Hillary whispered.

"I don't know," Jane whispered back. She reached for Hillary's hand. "But I'm sure of one thing. That is definitely the same man as the telephone repairman. Did you get a look at what he's wearing on his feet?"

"His boots? Yes. They were muddy."

"The same lizard-skin boots the telephone repairman was wearing."

"And the gas station attendant?" Hillary was holding Jane's hand in a tight grip, and Jane could sense that she was shaking.

"Same," Jane said.

"I'm afraid I don't know what this means," Hillary said.

"Neither do I," Jane said. "Not yet, anyway."

"What do you mean, not yet? We're not going to take this any farther are we? We're just going to leave this alone, not get involved. Jane this is too dangerous to—what are you doing?''

Jane didn't respond. She had let go of Hillary's hand and was feeling along the shelf again. When she found the box of matches, she handed it to Hillary. ''Light another match and hold it close to his face again,'' she said.

Hillary hesitated a moment, as if she was about to protest, but she struck the match on the side of the box. As the tiny flame flared, Jane leaned forward and studied the man's face.

''He looks just like Bruce did,'' Jane said. ''As if he'd had a heart attack. And he threw up. Remember that sour smell on Bruce?''

''You think he had a heart attack?'' Hillary seemed surprised. ''But he's so young.''

''Yes.'' Jane sounded distracted. ''Hillary,'' she said, turning to her just as she struck another match, ''what was it Katrin said foxglove is called? The scientific name, I mean.''

''Scientific name? I don't know. I was never very good at Latin. And why are you asking about foxglove at a time like this?''

Jane grabbed Hillary's hand again and steered her toward the staircase. ''Come on,'' she said. ''Let's go up to the library.''

''The library? At this hour?''

''It's better than this creepy place, isn't it?'' Jane said, pulling her along.

''You've got a point,'' Hillary said, once again following closely. ''But what are we going to do in the library?''

''I'm going to look up foxglove in one of Katrin's botany books.

They were climbing the steps cautiously, groping the walls as they ascended. ''Did you say foxglove?'' Hillary asked. ''Oh, I get it! You think it's poison. Well, you're wrong. It's a lovely plant, and there's nothing poisonous about it. Why would you . . .''

They had just reached the second landing, and they heard a screech that left Hillary in midsentence. She stifled a scream with a hand to her mouth, and Jane felt her heart leap in her chest.

There was a scurrying of something at their feet and then a familiar meow.

"What are you doing here, Hieronymus?" Jane stooped to pick up the cat, but she hissed and swatted a paw at her hand. Jane jumped back, bumping into Hillary.

"Leave her alone! Nasty old cat!" Hillary said.

Jane was inclined to oblige. She was in no mood for a battle with a cat. There were enough dangers of greater magnitude lurking about. She was beginning to worry about Lotus. Would they find her body next?

When they were back in Hillary's room, Hillary went immediately to the bed and sat down heavily.

"Are you all right?" Jane asked. Hillary looked pale and there were dark circles under her eyes. She definitely needed her makeup, but her stricken look went beyond needing a little foundation and blush.

"My Lord no, I'm not all right," Hillary said, with a hand to her forehead. Her broken nails made Jane feel sad. "I know it's different in California where you come from, but I'm just not used to finding dead bodies day after day."

"Hillary, nobody finds dead bodies day after day. Not even in California."

"Well, it *is* so much more, well, relaxed and permissive there."

"Killing people isn't permissive, Hillary. It's criminal," Jane said as she pushed the bureau against the wall to cover the passageway. She dusted her hands together. "And even California has laws."

Hillary shook her head stubbornly. "I know how it is in California, Jane. I've been there. Women wear shorts in the shopping malls, and some people don't even say grace before a meal."

Jane rolled her eyes. "I'm going to the library. You want to stay here and try to get some rest?"

Hillary sprang from the bed. "Stay here? Alone? With a killer on the loose?" She followed Jane out the door and stayed close beside her all the way down to the library.

They lit one of the lamps in the darkened room, and Jane took it with her, holding it close to the shelf from which she had seen Katrin pull one of her books earlier. She chose one entitled *The Properties of Common Garden Plants* and opened it to the index. She found foxglove and turned to the page number listed.

"This is it," Jane said. "It says it's called *Digitalis purpurea*. Yes, that's what Katrin called it." She glanced at Hillary. "And I think *digitalis* is the name of a heart medication, isn't it?"

Hillary shook her head. "I don't know, but so what if it is?"

Jane went back to reading the book. Listen to this, she said, reading aloud, " 'A genus of plants of the family scrophulariaceae. *Digitalis purpurea* has historically been used for medicinal purposes. Modern use isolates glycosides from the leaves for a medication, digitalis. . . .' " She glanced at Hillary. "See? I was right." She went back to reading " ' . . . digitalis, which strengthens the force of contraction of the heart, and, at the same time, slows the beat, allowing the heart muscle to rest even though working harder.' "

"I don't understand why you're reading this, Jane. A lot of plants are used as medicines, but what does that have to do with Bruce and Reverend Johnston?"

Jane didn't take her eyes from the page. "Wait, there's more. Listen to this: 'Humans and animals may be poisoned when relatively small amounts of the glycosides are introduced to the system, either through overdose of the drug or by ingesting the foliage of the plant. Symptoms include abdominal pain, nausea, vomiting, disturbed heartbeat, convulsions, and death.' "

Jane slammed the book closed. "So, I was right. Foxglove can be poison. And the symptoms sound suspiciously like what happened to Bruce and, I think, Reverend Johnston."

Hillary was, by this time, studying her face in the mirror that hung over the fireplace and patting her flat, stringy hair. "Jane, hon, are you jumping to conclusions? That's not like

you. Maybe we've been here too long.'' She turned to face
Jane. ''You have absolutely no proof that anyone was poi
soned, much less what they were poisoned with.''

''You're right, Hill, I don't. But think about it. The sher
iff said he thought Bruce died of a heart attack. The rev
erend looks as if he must have died the same way Bruce
died. Remember, we didn't find any marks on the body.''

Hillary frowned.

''Think about this,'' Jane said. ''Remember Katrin gath
ering all that foxglove? That's how you got the idea to
make the foxglove wreaths.''

''Oh my Lord! Katrin?'' Hillary whispered. She brough
a hand to cover her mouth. Then she frowned and shook
her head as if she was reconsidering it. ''Still, I don't know
There's no proof, and don't you think poisoning someone
seems a little—I don't know, melodramatic?''

''Kind of *Arsenic and Old Lace*, you mean?''

''*Arsenic and Old Lace*? Why Cassandra had the lead in
that.'' Jane and Hillary were both startled at the sound of
the voice coming from the shadows of the library. In the
next moment, Julia materialized out of the darkness. ''Cas
sandra was convincing in the part of an old lady in that
play. Such a talented child. Bruce and I saw her in it in
Birmingham. Now she's . . .'' Julia sat down on one of the
sofas and cried softly.

''Oh now, lamb,'' Hillary said, going to her. She sat
down next to her on the sofa. ''I know this has been just
awful for you, and now the bad news is . . .''

Jane was doing her best to signal Hillary not to say any
more by putting a finger to her pursed lips and shaking her
head. She had decided it would be best not to discuss the
reverend's death with any of the family members until she
had spoken to Sheriff Harkelrode.

Hillary got the message. ''What I mean is, the good news
is, time heals all wounds,'' Hillary crooned.

''But a heart attack? Bruce never had heart trouble. So
why did he . . . And Cassandra. So young. They said she
had a heart attack, too. How could that be? She was such
a bright young thing, and Lotus said she had a beau.'' Julia

smiled at Hillary. "Cassandra has never had a young man before. She was always so—well—caustic. But there was a young actor she met in one of those theaters in Birmingham where she was doing those plays. She had the lead in *Arsenic and Old Lace*, you know. Played an old lady."

"Yes, I know," Hillary assured her.

"You know? Oh! Did you see her? At the Old State Theater in Birmingham? Wasn't she wonderful? She's supposed to do *Ten Little Indians* next month. Bruce and I are going to see her. If you'd like to come with us . . ." Julia started to cry. "Oh dear, I don't suppose we will be doing that, will we?"

"Now, now." Hillary spoke in her most soothing voice. "Why don't you go to bed now, Julia?" She helped her up from the sofa.

"Bed? But I couldn't find Bruce, and I thought he might be in the library. He often comes down here to read, you know."

"Come along now," Hillary said, leading her toward the door. "I'll see if I can get you some nice hot milk." Hillary gave a knowing look to Jane as she led Julia out the door.

Jane watched them leave, feeling pity for Julia. Grief had left her confused and disoriented and slipping in and out of reality. Her mind was playing tricks, perhaps as a protective device, trying to take her back to a more pleasant reality when Bruce was alive and they could go to the theater together.

"Bruce and I used to like to see Wi-Wi-Winston perform, too, but then he went away," Julia said to Hillary. "I suppose he was doing a road show. But you can go with us to Birmingham to see Cassandra in *Ten Little Indians*. Bruce is so looking forward to it."

Jane shook her head, feeling suddenly very tired. All of this had to end sometime. For now, however, she had to call the sheriff and tell him about the body in the basement.

When she dialed the number, it was the night deputy who answered the phone. He identified himself as Melvin.

"You've got what? Another body at the Beans'?" Melvin said when Jane gave him the reason for her call. "Oh my God. Lonnie's already in bed. He ain't going to like this.''

"Nobody likes this," Jane said. There was weariness in her voice. "And listen, I have reason to believe my own life is in danger, as well as others.''

"Well, Lord, I'll tell Lonnie, but listen, he had barbecue for supper tonight, and when he has barbecue he gets a heartburn, and when he gets a heartburn he gets mean. He ain't going to like me waking him up." The deputy sounded worried.

"Life's not fair, Melvin," Jane said and hung up the phone. She started upstairs, hoping Melvin was calling Lonnie Harkelrode. She would tell him about Lotus being missing and the note she'd left when he arrived.

Hillary was in Jane's room when she opened the door, already in her borrowed nightgown, and just about to crawl into bed. "I hope you don't mind," she said, "but since there's another dead body down there, and Lotus said we were in danger, there's no way I'm going to sleep in that room alone.''

Jane locked the door. She was in no mood to be alone, either. She tried to push the dresser in front of the door. "Come on, Hillary, get up and help me."

Hillary got up reluctantly and was soon at Jane's side, pushing the dresser. "I take it this means you're scared, too.''

"I'm scared," Jane said.

Hillary looked as if she was about to cry.

"I still can't put all this together," Jane said. She told Hillary what she had learned from Chester about the Bean family's financial problems.

"So they're killing each other to get this place?" Hillary asked.

"Apparently," Jane said.

"But who? Who's doing the killing?"

"Katrin?"

"I still think you're wrong."

"Lotus?"

"Maybe," Hillary said, "but why did she try to warn us?"

"Good point." Jane sighed. "It could be Lizzie trying to protect her turf. Or Winston with the same motive Katrin or Lotus might have. Or even Julia, I guess. Or Cassandra."

"In other words, it could be anybody." Hillary shook her head. "I'm getting another headache, thinking about all of this, and I have to get some rest. I'll get bags under my eyes if I don't."

Hillary was in bed and asleep within a few minutes. Jane found herself staying awake, listening for the sound of the helicopter that meant the sheriff had arrived.

She had no idea that she had even been asleep when something awakened her: the all-too-familiar thumping sound. Hillary woke when Jane got out of bed.

"Where are you going?" Hillary's voice was hoarse with sleep.

"I heard something. I'm going to investigate." Dawn had given her courage.

"Not without me, you're not." Hillary scrambled out of bed and reached for her clothes. She was close behind Jane when they stepped out into the hall.

It was odd, Jane thought, that no sounds came from downstairs. Usually, the family was up by this hour. When they went downstairs, they found no one in the kitchen or dining room or in the library.

"This is odd," Jane said. "Where could they be?"

"Maybe in their rooms," Hillary said.

"Or in the cellar."

Hillary shook her head. "No!"

Jane took a deep breath and tried to summon her courage. "I'm going to have a look just to be sure. You wait here." She started for the door.

Hillary called out to her just as she reached the door. "Wait!"

Jane turned back to look at her.

"The sheriff will be here soon, won't he? Why not just let him look down there?"

"The sheriff should have been here last night. Who knows if he will ever show up. One of us has to go down there."

"But what if they're dead, like Bruce and Reverend Johnston?" Hillary looked very pale.

"What if they're not?"

"What do you mean?" Now Hillary looked ill, as if she might faint at any moment.

"What if they need our help, Hillary? We've got to go see. Come on. We'll take the outside entrance to the cellar so we won't have to find our way down that creepy passage again."

Hillary followed reluctantly as Jane walked through the house and out the back door to the cellar's entrance. She was surprised to see the cellar door open. She exchanged a glance with Hillary, who looked as uncertain as she felt. Jane started cautiously down the steps.

"Jane!" Hillary's voice had an urgent, frightened tone. "Don't go down there."

Jane ignored her and continued descending the steps. With the outside door open, the cellar wasn't as dark as it had been on the other occasions she'd been in it, but it was still shadowy. The would-be Reverend Johnston's body still lay where they'd found it.

The dank air of the cellar closed around Jane like a heavy cloak as she reached the bottom step. She turned around to see Hillary, looking worried, still waiting at the top of the steps.

"Hello?" Jane said in a quiet, timid voice. There was no response. She looked around her, seeing nothing except the body and the dusty shelves stocked with canned goods and an assortment of apparently little-used household items, "I don't think they're down here," she said over her shoulder to Hillary.

"Are you sure?" There was a pause. "All right then, I'm coming down. I don't like it up here all alone."

"Never mind, I'm coming up," Jane said. Just as she started to turn around, she saw what looked like a shadow in a corner. She took a step closer. By this time, Hillary was at her side.

"What are you—"

"Shhh!" Jane said, holding out a hand in caution to

Hillary. She took another step toward the shadow, and in the same instant heard an eerie moan that made her skin tingle and sent fear rolling down her spine.

Hillary screamed and grabbed Jane around her shoulders. There was another shadowy movement. Jane and Hillary stood immobilized; then the shadow began to take human form and Julia emerged from the shadows.

"Oh!" She brought a hand to her mouth.

"Julia? What are you doing down here?" Jane asked.

"Why, I was searching for—for everyone." She shook her head in a confused manner and looked as if she was about to cry. "I can't find Bruce or Cassandra or Winston or Katrin. Even Lizzie's gone. And Hieronymus, too. There's only that—that person there, sleeping." She pointed to the body.

Jane put her arms around the tiny woman and tried to lead her toward the stairs. "Julia, let's go back into the house. Maybe if you have a cup of tea . . ."

"I can't understand why Bruce is late for breakfast. He . . ." She looked at Jane with another puzzled expression. "Oh dear, Bruce won't be coming back, will he?"

"Julia . . ."

"Oh, now I remember," Julia said, as a brief light shown in her eyes. "I thought I heard Hieronymus. I came down here, looking for her, but she's not here. I'm *certain* I heard her."

"It's all right, Julia," Hillary said in a soothing tone. "Come on upstairs, and I'll fix you some tea."

Julia allowed herself to be led up the stairs and into the kitchen. When they entered, Hillary sucked in her breath once again in alarm.

"There!" She pointed to the counter next to the sink. "You see that?" She spoke in a hoarse whisper to Jane. "Foxglove! Katrin must have put it there."

Julia by this time had wandered off to the table and no longer seemed to realize Jane and Hillary were in the room with her. She sat down, still wearing her confused expression.

"Yes," Jane whispered back. "We may have found the murder weapon."

"And Katrin is the murderer," Hillary said. "I'm sure of it!"

Jane shook her head. "It doesn't fit."

Hillary snatched the teakettle from the stove and filled it with water. "What doesn't fit?"

Jane sat down at the table with Julia. "All these pieces to the puzzle. Katrin just isn't one of the pieces that fits."

Julia gave her a sweet smile.

"I don't see why not," Hillary said, rummaging in the cupboards for cups and tea bags. After all, there's that . . ." She moved her head and her eyes in an elaborate gesture to indicate the foxglove.

"Well there's that," Jane agreed, "but I still don't think Katrin is the key."

Hillary was opening cupboard doors and banging them shut. "Why can't I find any tea bags?"

Julia turned her attention to Hillary. "In the pantry, dear. There's the regular tea and the herbs that Lizzie uses for her special brews."

Hillary glanced at Julia. "Lizzie?" She gave Jane a knowing look. "Just plain Lipton tea bags will do fine, thank you. I wouldn't touch Lizzie's special brew for all the tea in China."

"But I don't know about a key." Julia now wore a puzzled look. "I don't think we ever lock the pantry."

Hillary opened the pantry door and quickly pulled out a box of tea bags. "That's it, Jane!" she whispered. "Lizzie! Lizzie brewed that foxglove. Lizzie is the key to all of this."

Jane shook her head.

"Who then?" Hillary gripped the box of tea bags until her knuckles turned white.

"Cassandra is the key," Jane said.

"Cassandra?" Hillary looked puzzzled.

"Oh, Cassandra's feeling ever so much better now," Julia said at the same time.

"Jane, you're jumping to conclusions. She may not stay

in her casket, but you have no proof she's murdering people,'' Hillary said, ignoring Julia.

"She said I mustn't worry about her,'' Julia said, wearing her faraway look. "But I don't think she has a key. Not to the pantry, at least.''

"I didn't say she was murdering people. I said she was the key to the mystery.'' Jane said.

Hillary gave the teakettle an impatient look. "Well, you're going to have a hard time asking her questions, under the circumstances.''

Jane was absently tracing a pattern on the oilcloth table cover with her finger, thinking Hillary was right. Thinking she'd have a hard time questioning anyone.

Julia was still talking. "Lotus likes those mysteries. You know, the ones with the cats? But Cassandra doesn't. Those two girls argue all the time.'' A puzzled frown matted her forehead. "I wonder where those two girls are? Have you seen them?''

"No, I'm afraid not, Julia,'' Jane said.

"They're usually around arguing about something,'' Julia said. "Cassandra's horoscope column or the cat or something.''

"It's all right, lamb.'' Hillary covered Julia's hand with her own. "Drink your tea now, you'll feel better. That's a girl!'' She glanced at Jane. "You still haven't come up with a *reason* for Cassandra to be pretending to be dead.''

"Oh, there are lots of reasons I can see now, thanks to Chester,'' Jane said. "To keep from paying debts. To keep from going to jail. To collect insurance money.''

Julia stood up suddenly, knocking over her teacup. "Oh no! You mustn't use that word!''

Hillary and Jane both gave Julia startled looks. Hillary stood and put her arm around Julia's shoulder. "What's wrong, dear?''

Julia seemed about to cry. "Lizzie says we mustn't talk about it,'' she whispered.

"Talk about what?'' Jane asked, standing to help Hillary get Julia seated again.

"Jane, she said she can't talk about it,'' Hillary scolded.

Julia brightened. "You mentioned insurance. I can talk about that. My late husband was an insurance salesman, you know. Did you know my late husband?"

"Bruce?" Jane said. "Yes, of course." She was helping Hillary clean up the spilled tea.

Julia set down her empty teacup from which she had been trying to drink. "You know him? Wonderful man, isn't he?"

Jane nodded. "The insurance salesman. You were saying you could talk about insurance, but not about, what? Jail?"

"Shhhh!" Julia seemed quite agitated again.

"Now, now," Hillary said as she set another cup of tea in front of Julia. She gave Jane a warning look. "We won't talk about the *J* word. We will talk about insurance if that's what you want to talk about."

"Insurance? What a coincidence. My husband sells insurance. Does yours sell it, too?"

"No, lamb." Hillary was still fussing about, pouring more hot water, looking for another tea bag, slicing more lemon.

"It's just as well," Julia said. "It's a difficult way to make a living. At least Bruce was able to sell policies to the family."

Jane sat up straighter. Julia had gotten her attention. "Did Cassandra have a policy?"

"Oh yes, and Lizzie and Katrin. Are you interested in insurance? I can have my husband contact you."

Jane tried to sound polite. "No, thank you," she said, then put her head in her hands and mumbled, "We've got to get out of here."

"Oh, please don't leave," Julia said. "Not until you've helped me find everyone. Including Hieronymus. I know that cat is here. I can hear her meow. If we find Hieronymus, we'll find Lotus and Cassandra. That cat's never very far away from one or the other." Julia began to cry.

"Oh, now, Julia," Hillary said, dabbing at her eyes with a napkin. "You mustn't cry." She turned to Jane. "You're upsetting her. Can't you see?"

"Oh, no, it's not her, dear," Julia said. She looked at

Jane. "Will you please find them for me? Bruce is late for breakfast." Julia pushed back from the table and stood. "I'll be in my room. When you find him, will you please send him up? I've had such an exhausting morning looking for everyone."

"Wait!" Jane said and grabbed her arm to stop her. "I don't think you should be alone. It's not safe."

"Of course it's safe," Julia said. She pulled herself free of Jane's grasp and moved away, ignoring their warnings.

"Lock your door!" Jane called after her. Jane and Hillary watched her leave.

"Poor soul," Hillary said, shaking her head.

"Oh my God!" Jane said.

"What?" Hillary glanced at Jane as if she was afraid something was wrong.

"I just realized. Julia makes sense."

"You worry me, Jane."

"She does!" Jane sounded breathless with excitement. "At least part of the time." She started for the door. "Come on, Hillary."

"What . . . Where are we going?" Hillary asked, hurrying after her.

"To find Hieronymus."

"You don't like that cat, Jane."

"That's beside the point. I have a hunch Julia is right. When we find the cat, we'll find Lotus or Cassandra. Maybe both." Jane started for the stairway.

"The last time we saw Hieronymus she was in that secret passage," Hillary said. "And Lotus and Cassandra weren't there."

"We can't be sure of that," Jane said. She was bounding up the staircase.

"Wait!" Hillary called, trying to keep up as Jane hurried down the hall to Hillary's room. "Of course we can be sure they weren't there. We didn't see anyone in that stairwell except Hieronymus."

"Not in the stairwell," Jane said, tugging at the bureau. "In the wall."

"In the wall?" Hillary threw up her hands. "Jane, you have lost it."

Once the bureau had been moved aside, Jane lit the lamp and took it with her as she started down the stairs. "I haven't lost it, I'm just beginning to figure it out. At least part of it." When they reached the second landing, Hieronymus was still there, sitting on her haunches, eyes alert. Jane set the lamp on the landing and once again ran her hands along the wall.

"What are you doing?" Hillary was hovering over her, and she sounded edgy.

"Feeling for an opening again. I don't think that light we saw was from a bedroom. I think there's another room or secret compartment or something back there."

"Oh Lord, how do you know?"

"Hieronymus told me."

"You're scaring me, Jane."

"Look at her. She's sitting there as if she's waiting for someone to come out. She knows Lotus is in there, and I have a hunch Cassandra is, too." Jane tapped softly at the wall. "I think she was pretending to be dead, maybe to collect the insurance money for herself and her lover. Only something went wrong. Someone else had a claim to that money and killed her lover for it."

"Her lover? Who's her lover? You're losing me, Jane." Hillary, by now, had joined Jane in feeling along the wall.

"The Reverend Johnston."

"No!"

"Yes. Only he wasn't a minister. Or a telephone repairman or gas station attendant, either; although he was pretending to be. I think he was the actor Julia said Cassandra fell in love with."

"But why was he pretending to be all those people? And why was he killed?" She frowned. "Are you sure he wasn't the escaped convict?"

"Reasonably sure," Jane said. "But there are a lot of answers I don't know, and I think some of the answers will be behind this wall." Her fingers sensed a crack in the wall,

long and narrow and very even. "I think I found something!"

"What?" Hillary was excited.

"I'm not sure. An opening maybe." She tried to get her
fingers into the crack to pry it apart, but it was too narrow.
In frustration, she kicked at the wall, and when she did, a
portion of it swung back. Hieronymus screeched and ran
into the opening, and Jane caught a glimpse of three figures
seated in a small space. In almost the same moment, a draft
from below swept up the stairway and the lamp she had
set behind her on the landing went out. Hillary screamed,
and Jane turned around when she heard footsteps on the
stairway.

15

The footsteps stopped, and there was deadly silence. Finally, they heard a rustling on the stairs below them.

"Who is it?" Hillary whispered.

"I think it's the murderer," Jane whispered back.

"Oh my Lord, do you know who it is?"

"Winston?" Jane called aloud. "Winston, is that you?" The only answer was a frantic rustling.

"Winston, if you turn yourself in now, it will be easier for you."

"I'm not going back!" It was Winston's voice.

"Not going back where?" Hillary whispered. She was holding onto Jane's arm with a frightened grip.

"Prison," Jane whispered back. "Winston, you've already committed two murders, don't compound it by—"

A shot rang out before she could finish her sentence, and she felt the bullet whiz past her head. Hillary screamed, and they both dropped to the floor, hovering in squatting positions against each other. Jane heard a frantic, muffled mumbling coming from inside the tiny room.

"What are we going to do?" Hillary's whispering voice was choked with fear.

"Shhh," Jane said, then whispered, "Give me one of your earrings."

"What?"

"Give it to me!" She held Hillary's knee, and Hillary removed an earring and placed it with trembling hands into Jane's palm. Jane then tossed it down the steps. The response was immediate, a brief rustling, and then another shot. "He's still there," Jane whispered.

Jane stood and started cautiously down the darkened stairway. She heard the rustling again, the sound of feet on the steps retreating.

"Jane, come back," Hillary called.

As she continued to advance a few more steps, she heard a thud and knew that Winston had jumped over the railing to the stairs below.

"Winston!" she called again. Another bullet zipped past her.

"Jane!" She heard Hillary's frantic cry as she once again crouched down. She waited several seconds before she heard another sound. Probably the cellar door opening, she thought. She stood slowly and made her way back to Hillary.

"Jane, are you all right?" Hillary asked, when Jane had joined her.

"Yes, but now we've got to help the others." She and Hillary made their way into the darkened chamber with their hands in front of them, feeling for obstacles and using the muffled cries to help guide them. Jane's hand fell upon fleshy arms. "Lotus! Just a minute, I'll get you untied." She felt for the handkerchief around her mouth and slipped it off.

"Oh thank God, thank God!" Lotus said. Her voice was tearful. "I was afraid he was coming back to kill us. My hands, get my hands, then we'll untie the others. Where's that lamp?" she said when her hands were free. She scooped Hieronymus up in her arms. "I have matches in my pocket. I always carry them because the electricity in this damn place is always going off."

Lotus felt for Jane's hand and gave her the matches, then

Jane made her way back to the landing to find the lamp. When it was lit, she held it up and saw that Katrin was tied to another chair with a gag around her mouth, and a third woman she assumed to be Cassandra was tied and gagged in yet another. She looked like the picture that appeared with the horoscope column in the *Prosper Picyune*: thirty-something with a round face and a lot of tightly permed blond hair. The same person they'd seen in the casket.

"We've got to get to Willie," the woman said as soon as her gag was off. Hillary was trying to untie her hands.

"Cassandra!" Lotus was alarmed. "Watch what you're saying!"

"For Christ's sake, Lotus. It doesn't matter now." Cassandra said.

"Stop it, you two," Katrin said. "At least when I thought Cassie was dead, we didn't have to put up with all this quarreling."

At the same time, Hillary dropped her hands from the rope she was trying to untie and took a step back. Jane could see, even in the dim light, that her face was pale. "You're Cassandra?" Hillary asked.

"Get these damn ropes off of me!" Cassandra was trying to wriggle herself free, almost toppling the chair in the process.

"She's not dead, Hillary," Jane said, helping with the ropes. "She's very much alive, just as we thought. And Winston's name isn't really Winston, is it, Cassandra?" she said as the last rope dropped. "It's Willie. Willie Peabody."

"Oh Lord, help us," Katrin said.

"Willie Peabody, alias Winston Bean," Jane said. "An escaped convict and a would-be actor, just like the so-called Reverend Johnston was. You got both of them mixed up in some kind of get-rich-quick scheme. It must have been the life insurance policy Bruce had sold you. And you must have killed Bruce when he caught on to your scheme, and the reverend, too, so you could make off with all the money."

"My God, Cassandra, is that true?" Katrin was staring at her, aghast.

"No! No!" Cassandra was crying hard. "It wasn't like that at all. I didn't kill anybody, I swear I didn't. It was Willie. Willie got greedy." She turned suddenly to Lotus. "You told her all this, didn't you? You couldn't keep your mouth shut, you bitch!"

"Oh my!" Hillary said, obviously shocked by Cassandra's language.

"I didn't!" Lotus said, shaking her head and stroking Hieronymus. "I didn't say a thing, I swear."

"No, she didn't," Jane assured her. "In fact, I wasn't at all certain I had it all figured out until just now, when you confirmed it."

"You tricked me! You tricked me into confessing." Cassandra looked frightened.

"You're the master of tricks, Cassandra," Jane said. "Pretending to be dead. Enlisting actors to help you."

"And pretending to be a ghost!" Lotus sounded disgusted. She turned to Jane. "I didn't know about her stupid trick when you first got here, honest. I thought she was dead. I thought someone had killed her because I saw someone coming out of her room. I thought it was America Elizabeth. Now I know it was Cassandra herself." She turned back to Cassandra. "I told her it was crazy as soon as I found out about it. I told her it wouldn't work."

"It worked for Virginia Blaylock." Cassandra sounded defensive.

"Have you never had an original thought of your own, Cassandra?" Lotus still did nothing to hide her disgust. "And now you're in big trouble because of all these murders. Poor Uncle Bruce. And Jason, too!"

It wasn't my idea to take it this far. It was Cousin Willie's idea, and you should be glad I never told him what you know, Lotus. He might have killed you the way he killed Uncle Bruce and Jason. If you hadn't been so nosy and eavesdropped on everyone, you wouldn't have been involved." Cassandra's fear had given her voice a whining quality. "You've all got to believe me. No one was supposed to die. I certainly didn't want Jason dead." She began to cry. "We would have both escaped if it hadn't been for that storm."

"The storm?" Hillary seemed confused.

Cassandra nodded, sniffling. "Jason was already here on the grounds when the storm hit. I was standing out on the balcony looking for him that night, but I couldn't see much because of the weather. That's why he had to dream up that telephone repairman scheme to get in the house. Now I wish he hadn't made it at all," she wailed. "He wouldn't be dead now if he'd just stayed on the other side of the bridge."

"Then it was Jason who tried to kill us," Hillary said. "With those garden shears."

"Jason wouldn't kill anyone," Cassandra said. "That was Cousin Willie. He was trying to scare you away."

"*Cousin* Willie?" Hillary sounded confused.

"Yes, he's our cousin," Lotus said. "You might as well know the truth. He's been in prison for two years, only we never could talk about it. Aunt Lizzie forbade it. She said we must never mention it because it brought shame to the Beans, even though he's from the Peabody side, and only a second cousin three times removed."

"Twice," Katrin said. "Twice removed."

Lotus gave a dismissive wave with her pudgy hand. "Whatever. Anyway, we couldn't talk about his being in prison, and when he escaped, we couldn't talk about that, either. It was Aunt Lizzie's idea that we call him Winston Bean when you two got trapped here by the storm, and of course we did. All of us. Even Katrin."

"What else could I do?" Katrin looked stricken and pale. "Aunt Lizzie demanded it." She turned to Jane. "Aunt Lizzie has always told us all she would cut us out of her will if we didn't do as she says. You don't know what it's like having her control your life that way. This is her house. Her land. We're all trapped here. And there's no one to inherit it. No daughter of a daughter. Aunt Lizzie was the last."

"She's right," Cassandra said. She started for the stairs.

"I had to get away from this," she said over her shoulder as the others followed her out. "That's why I came up with that scheme to play dead. Jason and I were going to take the insurance money and run away to Hollywood."

"You came up with the scheme?" Lotus was indignant. "You came up with nothing. You stole Virginia's idea."

"The coroner's report," Jane interrupted. "I suppose you got Willie to forge it, saying you died of a heart attack. It must have looked authentic enough for Sheriff Harkelrode to believe it."

"I never said Willie wasn't good at what he does. But now he's gone and killed Jason, the only man I ever loved." She had begun to sob again.

"Jason. Is that the reverend's real name?" Hillary asked as they made their way down the stairs to the basement.

"He's not a reverend. He's an actor," Cassandra said. She wiped her eyes with the back of her hand.

"He played the part of a gas station attendant very well. And of a minister, too, but the telephone repairman needs work." Hillary was serious about her critique.

"He was only working at that gas station until he got his break in serious acting." Cassandra was defensive now. "And he had to pretend to be a telephone repairman to get in the house. Aunt Lizzie would never have let him in otherwise. And he had to come in to help me. Poor Jason, he was staying out in the woods, and I went out in the rain looking for him. Cousin Willie talked him into playing the part of the minister. And then he killed him." She sobbed as she climbed out the cellar door.

"You and—what's his name? Jason? The two of you thought this up? The idea of pretending to be dead to get the insurance money? Now I'm confused," Jane said, following her, along with the others. "I thought you said it was Willie who came up with the scheme."

Cassandra turned around to face her and a look passed over her face, like that of a frightened animal. "All right, it was my idea. At least, at first. But I couldn't figure out how to make it look like I was officially dead or how to get the money, since Aunt Lizzie was the beneficiary. So I visited Cousin Willie in prison. I knew he was clever enough to figure something out for us. He knows Jason, of course, from the theater in Birmingham and from the gas station where he worked. Anyway, he said I should make him the beneficiary, and he would share the money with us. Then he would get a fake death certificate to send to the insurance company. Cousin Willie's good at that. He went to prison for counterfeiting. He got caught once, but he's still good at it.''

''So half the money was what he was supposed to get out of this?'' Jane asked.

''That and his freedom,'' Cassandra said. ''We, uh, sort of helped him escape.''

Katrin gasped. Lotus looked sad as she stroked Hieronymus.

''It wasn't hard, really,'' Cassandra said. She had started walking away again. ''Cousin Willie worked in the prison kitchen, and Jason dressed up like a delivery man and drove in. Getting the truck inside the prison yard was the hard part, but Jason was a wonderful actor.''

''You tricked all of us?'' Katrin said. She sounded angry.

Cassandra shrugged. ''It was easy. Except for Lotus, of course. Miss Nosy!'' She gave her an angry look. ''You and your eavesdropping!''

Lotus gave her a noncommittal shrug. ''I told you I didn't really want to know.'' She pulled Hieronymus to her ample bosom, as if for comfort. ''In fact, I wish I hadn't.''

''Why didn't you tell someone the truth once you found out?'' Jane asked.

Lotus looked down at her feet and didn't answer. Cassandra laughed. ''Because I told her I would turn my column over to her if she kept her mouth shut. You've always been jealous of my column, haven't you, Lotus?''

''Your column!'' Lotus screeched. ''You don't know a thing about the stars. It was always really my column all along.''

''But I was the one who was smart enough to sell the idea to the newspapers.''

"It isn't smart to contract to do something you don't know how to do!"

"Will the two of you stop it!" Katrin said. "We've barely escaped death at the hands of Cousin Willie, and you two are bickering about a stupid horoscope column!"

"You're sure Winston—er, Willie was going to kill you?" Hillary asked.

Cassandra nodded. "I told you he got greedy. He killed Uncle Bruce when he found out, then he killed poor Jason so he wouldn't have to split the money with him." She began to cry again. "He was going to kill me and Lotus next, but he knew we were onto his awful witch's brew, and I wouldn't drink it the way Uncle Bruce and Jason did. He told Uncle Bruce it would help his hangover, and he told me just minutes ago that he got Jason to drink it by telling him it would—well, you know." She sniffed and cried harder

"What?" Jane asked.

Cassandra looked miserable. "He told him—it—would—increase his—you know," she said between sobs.

"Oh my!" Hillary said again.

"Why did he tie all of you up and leave you here?" Jane asked. "Why didn't he just kill you some other way?"

"He was going to," Katrin said. "I heard the two of them, Cousin Cassandra and Cousin Willie, arguing in the kitchen, and when I went to see what was going on . . . I tell you, I almost had a heart attack when I saw Cassandra alive. Lotus, you must have heard them, too, because you came in right behind me."

"That's right," Lotus said. "He had that gun, and he forced us all into this old room." She glanced at Cassandra and Katrin, a look of innocence brightening her pudgy face. Remember how we used to play in there when we were kids? Our great-great-grandfather had it built to hide the family from the Yankees during the War Between the States. There's a secret passage from one of the bedrooms, too."

"Really?" Jane and Hillary said together, glancing at each other.

"He would have killed us if you two hadn't scared him,"
Lotus said. "He must have thought you had a gun. I don't
know. He was just acting awfully nervous. Anyway, he was
going to kill Cassandra for the money and Katrin and me
because we'd learned the truth, and then he said he was
going after Aunt Lizzie because she would eventually know
the truth. I suppose he would get around to Aunt Julia, too,
even though she's so forgetful and harmless."

"And he didn't think Lizzie was harmless?" Jane asked.

"Aunt Lizzie?" Cassandra said. "Oh no. Aunt Lizzie
had the same power over him that she did everyone else.
She was threatening to turn him in to the police if he didn't
do it himself right away."

By this time, Cassandra had led the entourage to the front
of the house. "Damn!" she said. "Willie took the car."

"Where do you think he went?" Hillary asked.

"He went looking for Aunt Lizzie, of course," Cassandra said. "And we've got to find her first. Before he kills
her."

"We'll take my car," Hillary said. "Get in. All of you."

"Wait!" Jane said. "Why don't you let me dri—" It
was too late. Hillary was already getting in the driver's side,
and the others were getting in the car. Jane hesitated. "I
think we should call the sheriff. I can't understand why he
hasn't come." She glanced back at the house. "I'm going
to try to call him again."

"It won't do any good," Katrin said, stopping her.
"Willie cut the phone lines when Aunt Lizzie tried to call
the sheriff."

With a resigned sigh, Jane got in the front seat next to
Lotus, who was still holding Hieronymus.

"I should have gone to the police long ago," Lotus said
in a tearful voice. "I should never have let you bully me
into keeping my mouth shut, Cassandra." In spite of the
fact that she was speaking to Cassandra, who was in the
backseat, she kept her eyes straight ahead. Her head, along
with everyone else's, jerked back suddenly when Hillary
took off with a mighty revving of her engine. Hieronymus
let out a screech.

"Bully you?" Cassandra said in the middle of the head jerking. "I never bullied you. You're just as greedy as any of the rest of us. You wanted that column, and you'd do anything for it."

"I would not! I would not do just anything," Lotus said.

"My God, we're headed straight for that tree," Katrin cried.

"Where to?" Hillary asked, swerving just as she got to the tree at the end of the driveway.

"That way." Cassandra pointed into the woods.

Hillary gunned the motor, turning the Cadillac at the same time. Tree branches swatted at the windshield when she turned, and the right side of the car heaved up as she ran over a rather large tree stump.

"Lord help us," Katrin said at the same time that Cassandra and Lotus sucked in their breath. Jane merely closed her eyes and held on to the dashboard for dear life.

"Why do you think Lizzie would be in the woods?" Hillary asked. She seemed oblivious to anyone's fear.

"Why, to get away from Willie, of course," Cassandra said.

"Yes," Lotus said, agreeing with Cassandra for once. "She would go there to hide. She knows these woods like she knows her own house. Maybe America Elizabeth will help her." Lotus's large body pressed Jane against the door when Hillary turned a very sharp corner.

"America Elizabeth?" Jane's voice sounded choked because of the heavy weight pressing against her.

"She haunts the woods," Katrin, Cassandra, and Lotus said together. "Ouch!" added Katrin when her head hit the roof of the car as Hillary hit a bump in the road at a fast speed.

Hillary took her eyes off the road to turn around to the backseat, although she didn't reduce her speed. "Ya'll seen her?"

"Hillary! A deer just walked out of the woods. There! Front of you!" Jane screamed.

Hillary slammed on her brakes, throwing everyone forward and missing the frightened deer only by inches, then lurched along the road into the woods.

"Look!" Hillary said, pointing to her left. "I think I just saw someone.

"Where?" everyone asked at once.

"There! I saw it again." Hillary had once again taken her eyes off the road, this time veering to the left until the car suddenly tilted slightly forward, jerked, then came to a stop. Hillary gunned the motor, but nothing happened.

"Oh dear!" Hillary said. "What could be wrong? I've never had trouble with this car before."

"You're stuck, that's all," Katrin said. "This Alabama clay is easy to get a car stuck in when it's wet like it is now."

"Oh dear!" Hillary said again.

Jane was still watching the figure they'd seen running through the woods. "Look!" she cried. "I think that's Winston. I mean Willie. And he still has a gun."

At just that moment, the loud report of a gun echoed through the woods.

"Aunt Lizzie!" Katrin said.

"We've got to stop him!" Cassandra said.

Lotus was holding on to Hieronymus so tightly, the cat let out another angry screech.

The Cadillac's back doors opened, and Cassandra and Katrin got out. "No!" Jane called to them. "Don't go running after him. This could be dangerous!"

It was too late. The two of them were already running toward the spot where they had last seen Willie, and within seconds, they were out of sight, obscured by a heavy growth of pine trees. Another shot rang out and then a scream.

"Oh my God!" Jane said, opening her door and scrambling out of the car. She ran toward the woods, then slowed to a cautious walk. It was slow going in the rugged, hilly terrain, however, and she fell to her knees. Just as she pulled herself up, she saw a movement at a distance in front of her, and in the next moment, she knew it was Willie. He was brandishing a gun. As she moved a little closer, she saw that he was holding Katrin and a cowering Cassandra at gunpoint. Lizzie lay on the ground in a crumpled heap in front of them.

Jane halted, trying to think what to do. She couldn't afford to startle him and run the risk of him killing one or more of the three captives. While she hesitated, a noise behind her—voices and scrambling feet—attracted her attention. She turned around quickly and saw that it was Hillary and Lotus stumbling up the hill and through the trees.

"Stop where you are!" It was Willie's voice. He had heard the noise as well. "Stop where you are," he said again, with the gun still trained on Cassandra, Katrin, and Lizzie, "or I'll kill all of them."

They stopped. Waited. Jane felt as if her breath had turned to fire in her chest.

"Throw your weapon out there between us," Willie said.

"We have no weapon," Jane said.

Willie looked nervous, uncertain. "All right." His voice was shaking. "Come down here one at a time. Jane first."

Jane took a careful step toward him, and then another and another. Her heart flailed at her chest like a pendulum gone crazy.

"Over there," Willie said, motioning with the gun for Jane to stand with Cassandra and Katrin. When she was next to them, she dropped her eyes to look at Lizzie. She was moaning and writhing in obvious pain, but she seemed to be alive.

"Now you, Cousin Lotus," he said.

She obeyed, and so did Hillary.

When they were all standing together, Willie seemed to relax a little. He laughed. "This is going to be easy," he said. "Like shooting ducks, as they say."

"You won't get away with this," Jane said. "Six dead bodies in the woods? They'll be after you in no time."

"Shut up!" Willie said. "It didn't have to come to this, you know. If you and your flaky friend hadn't been so nosy. And if you hadn't been such a quivering fool about killing old Bruce, Cassandra."

"What about Jason?" Cassandra cried. "You didn't have to kill him, did you? Except for greed. You wanted it all for yourself. I would have been next, I know it!"

Willie laughed again. "You're slow, but you do finally catch on, don't you, dear cousin?"

"Is this worth it, Willie?" Jane asked. "How are you going to collect the money? The minute Willie Peabody puts in a claim, the cops will be onto you."

"Willie Peabody? Who's that?" Willie had a smirk on his face. "The beneficiary is Winston Bean. And I have the Social Security card and birth certificate I need to prove I'm Mr. Bean. Modern computerized presses are marvelous things." He looked at each of them, still wearing his smirk, then brought his eyes back to Jane. "You're first," he said. He raised his gun and leveled it at her head.

Jane wasn't sure her legs were going to hold her up, and she reached for Hillary's hand and squeezed it.

Hillary sucked in her breath audibly and pointed to the left. "Look!"

Willie diverted his eyes from Jane to glance in the direction Hillary had pointed.

"Wild onions!" Hillary said. "They're marvelous in salads and sauces, but I can never find them."

Jane used the moment to lunge at Willie, grasping for the gun. Willie struggled to hold on to the weapon. He pulled away, but Jane held on, grappling with him. Suddenly, a shot exploded, and Jane felt a burning in her shoulder, but she refused to let go. She pulled hard, toppling backward, but she had the gun, holding on with both hands. She sat up quickly, bringing her torso forward. Willie was in front of her, crouching, but he was being careful, afraid of the gun she now had trained on him.

Jane managed to get to her feet. "Stand up!" she barked, keeping the weapon leveled on Willie. The pain in her shoulder was becoming more intense, and she saw spots dancing in front of her eyes. She wasn't sure how long she could hang on. Willie made a slight move toward her, perhaps sensing her weakening. "Stay where you are!" she said. She felt as if her knees would buckle at any minute.

"That's right! Stay where you are!" a voice said from somewhere to her right. Jane was afraid to turn her head, but within seconds, Sheriff Harkelrode stepped out of the woods. Jane was surprised to see that Beau Jackson was only a step behind him, and they both had guns drawn.

There was a blur of activity in front of her. Bodies struggling with each other, another shot, Hillary falling to the ground, and then darkness.

EPILOGUE

The light was golden, but it had a blue halo, and there was music coming from somewhere. Jane closed her eyes again, lulled by the peacefulness, then opened them suddenly. What had happened? Was she dead? Was this what heaven was like?

Her eyes focused slowly on a square-jawed face with hazel eyes and dark brown hair.

"Beau?"

"You all right, hon?"

She tried to sit up. "Where am I? Where's Hill—"

Firm hands pushed her back. "You're in the hospital emergency room. Hillary's in the next cubicle."

"Hillary? Is she—"

"She's all right," Beau said, pushing her down again. "She just fainted, that's all. When she saw the blood all over you."

"What happened? Did I—"

"The escaped con, he shot you in the shoulder. You lost some blood, and you must have fainted, too, but the bullet came out clean."

Jane looked down at her bandaged arm. "And Willie? Did you get him?"

Beau smiled. "You got him, hon. We just did the cleanup work. You did the rest. Willie's in custody. Be back in prison in no time."

"But why didn't Harkelrode come when I called earlier?"

Beau put a soothing hand on her hand. "He tried to get there the night you called, but the bridge still wasn't fixed, and he told me the helicopter was broken."

"And you came, too. I didn't expect—"

"I called Harkelrode because I was worried about you. When he told me what was going on, I drove out there as fast as I could."

Jane nodded. "I still don't know how you knew to come into the woods. There was no one at the house to tell you."

"That's because Harkelrode got a call from Miss Bean. Miss Lizzie Bean. She called from the Collins's house. Seems her phone line had been cut. Mrs. Collins told us she'd be out in the woods."

"Lizzie!" Jane said. She tried to sit up again. "Is she all right?

"Yes, she's all right, too," Beau said, giving her another gentle push to keep her in bed. "Willie knocked her around some. Bruised her up, but she'll be all right. So is everyone else—except that one called Cassandra is facing charges for insurance fraud and aiding a prison escape."

A nurse stuck her head around the curtain that enclosed the emergency room cubicle where Jane was confined. "There's someone here to see you," she said. A blond head popped up from behind her, about even with her waist.

"Sarah!

"Mommy! Oh Mommy, are you OK?"

"I'm fine, Sarah." She stroked her hair. "But how did you get here?"

"Beau brought me," she said, looking up at him. "He met me at our house when Daddy brought me back. Oh, Mommy, I was so scared when they told me you were here."

"I'm fine, honey. But what about you? Did you enjoy your visit?"

Sarah shrugged. "It was OK, I guess. But I missed you, Mom, I really did."

"I missed you, too, Sarah. I want to hear all about your long weekend. Everything you did."

"But I want to hear about you first, Mom. Tell me what happened."

"There'll be plenty of time for that later," the nurse said. "For now, we've got to get you ready to get out of here. The doctor has released you, Mrs. Ferguson. You're going home. But I want you to take this first. For the pain." She handed her a tablet and a glass of water and stood over her until she swallowed it.

"It'll be a few minutes," the nurse said to Beau in a crisp voice. "We have some paperwork to take care of, so if you and the little girl could just wait in the lobby . . ."

Beau chuckled. "She was supposed to be waiting in the lobby until I found out if it was all right for her to come in, but I see she has a mind of her own. Just like her mother." He squeezed Jane's hand. "We'll be waiting out front," he said, then took Sarah's hand and led her out.

Jane watched them until they disappeared from her view, then she breathed a long sigh and closed her eyes, realizing now that she felt very tired and a little weak. They dumped you out of hospitals too soon these days. But then, she would have wanted it that way, anyway—to be home with Sarah. Maybe she'd ask Beau to spend the night. Their relationship hadn't progressed beyond his sleeping on the couch, though.

She began now to feel very relaxed. Yes, it would be good to get home.

"Jane?" The sound of someone calling her name startled her out of her half-sleep. She opened her eyes to see Hillary standing next to her bed, still looking bedraggled. "Jane, are you all right, lamb?"

"I'm fine, Hillary. The bullet apparently didn't do any permanent damage. Just lost a little blood, that's all."

"Oh Lord, I was worried. Lotus was, too. She said to give you her best."

"That was nice of her."

"She said to tell you you're very smart to have figured out Willie and Cassandra's scheme."

"It was mostly just lucky guesses, Hill." Jane's voice sounded weary, even to her own ears.

"There's one thing that hasn't been cleared up, though," Hillary said.

Jane nodded. "You're talking about America Elizabeth."

"Yes," Hillary said. "Do you think she was who I saw through the window of the tool shed that night in the cemetery?"

"I don't know. I thought it could have been Katrin or Lotus, but you know the Beans deny that. They insist it was the ghost of America Elizabeth." Jane sighed, a weary sound. "I'm just glad we don't have to deal with the Beans anymore."

Hillary twisted a strand of her unkempt hair around one of her fingers from which the polish had flaked off part way. "Well . . ." She wouldn't look at Jane.

"What is it, Hillary? What are you saying?"

"It will be quite simple, I'm sure. No problem at all, this time."

"What will be simple?"

"Lotus's party. She's thinking of having a little celebration to commemorate the fact that she will now have her own byline on the horoscope column."

Jane rolled her eyes. "Oh shit!"

"Jane, now, listen to me. It's worth celebrating. She can use the income to help take care of Aunt Lizzie and Aunt Julia, and it will be different this time. It will—"

"Mrs. Scarborough," a nurse said, sticking her head through the curtain. "Oh, there you are. Your husband is here to pick you up."

"Billy's here?"

"He's waiting in the car for you. Just out those double doors," the nurse said, pointing toward doors Jane couldn't see.

"We'll talk about this later," Hillary said, hurrying out. "Billy got me an appointment at the beauty parlor. Manicure, shampoo, set. The works.'' She waved her hand. ''We'll talk later.''

As Hillary left, she dropped the newspaper she'd been carrying under her arm on Jane's bed. While Jane waited for the nurse to come back to release her, she picked up the paper and paged through it, awkwardly because of her wounded shoulder. Her eyes fell upon the horoscope column. She searched out the section for Leo and read it.

The spirit of Susan B. Anthony speaks to you. Listen carefully. More adventure awaits you around the corner. Be alert for it.

The painkiller took hold, and Jane was asleep by the time she read the third sentence.

Elizabeth Daniels Squire

Peaches Dann is "memorable!"
—Sharyn McCrumb

Is There a Dead Man in the House?

Peaches's father and his new wife, Azalea Marlowe, were in Tennessee to oversee the renovation of Azalea's family home. Peaches finds the excavation process fascinating—almost like watching the house's memory come to life.

But some of the house's memories are less than pleasant, as proven by the discovery of century-old buried bones...and Azalea's fall from a broken ladder hints that violence may visit this house again...

__ 0-425-16142-0/$5.99

Whose Death Is It, Anyway?

While promoting her book, *How to Survive Without a Memory*, a family secret comes to light: Peaches learns that her cousin's daughter Kim is missing—and presumed dead. And if there's any hope for a future family reunion, it's up to Peaches to provide it...

__ 0-425-15627-3/$5.99

Memory Can Be Murder
__ 0-425-14772-X/$5.99

BERKLEY
PRIME
CRIME